Ken Follett
Eye of the Needle

"EXCELLENT . . .
a fascinating cat-and-mouse game
that leaves the reader suspended as
the book speeds to a breathless finale."
Denver Post

"SPELLBINDING . . .
top-notch suspense . . . a terrific thriller."
Miami Herald

"ONE OF THE WORLD'S GREAT
SPY NOVELISTS."
San Francisco Chronicle

"FOLLETT IS AN ARTIST OF
COMPELLING TALENTS."
Philadelphia Inquirer

"TENSE AND SUSPENSEFUL."
USA Today

"AN IMMENSELY SUCCESSFUL NAIL-BITER."
Milwaukee Sentinel

KEN FOLLETT

EYE OF THE NEEDLE

AVON BOOKS
An Imprint of HarperCollinsPublishers

AVON BOOKS
An Imprint of HarperCollins*Publishers*
10 East 53rd Street
New York, New York 10022-5299

First Avon Books paperback printing: August 2000

Avon Trademark Reg. U.S. Pat. Off. and in Other Countries, Marca
Registrada, Hecho en U.S.A.
HarperCollins® is a trademark of HarperCollins Publishers Inc.

Printed in the U.S.A.

　　　10　9　8　7　6　5　4　3

Acknowledgment

My thanks to Malcolm Hulke
for invaluable help,
generously given.

Preface

EARLY IN 1944 GERMAN INTELLIGENCE WAS PIECING together evidence of a huge army in southeastern England. Reconnaissance planes brought back photographs of barracks and airfields and fleets of ships in the Wash; General George S. Patton was seen in his unmistakable pink jodhpurs walking his white bulldog; there were bursts of wireless activity, signals between regiments in the area; confirming signs were reported by German spies in Britain.

There was no army, of course. The ships were rubber-and-timber fakes, the barracks no more real than a movie set; Patton did not have a single man under his command; the radio signals were meaningless; the spies were double agents.

The object was to fool the enemy into preparing for an invasion via the Pas de Calais, so that on D-Day the Normandy assault would have the advantage of surprise.

It was a huge, near-impossible deception. Literally thousands of people were involved in perpetrating the trick. It would have been a miracle if none of Hitler's spies ever got to know about it.

Were there any spies? At the time people thought they were surrounded by what were then called Fifth Columnists. After the war a myth grew up that MI5 had rounded up the lot by Christmas 1939. The truth seems to be that there were very few; MI5 did capture nearly all of them.

But it only needs one . . .

It is known that the Germans saw the signs they were meant to see in East Anglia. It is also known that they suspected a trick, and that they tried very hard to discover the truth.

That much is history. What follows is fiction.

Still and all, one suspects something like this must have happened.

Camberley, Surrey
June 1977

The Germans were almost completely deceived—only Hitler guessed right, and he hesitated to back his hunch . . .

A. J. P. Taylor
English History 1914–1945

PART
ONE

1

IT WAS THE COLDEST WINTER FOR FORTY-FIVE YEARS.
Villages in the English countryside were cut off by the
snow and the Thames froze over. One day in January
the Glasgow-London train arrived at Euston twenty-four
hours late. The snow and the blackout combined to make
motoring perilous; road accidents doubled, and people told
jokes about how it was more risky to drive an Austin Seven
along Piccadilly at night than to take a tank across the Sieg-
fried Line.

Then, when the spring came, it was glorious. Barrage
balloons floated majestically in bright blue skies, and soldiers on leave flirted with girls in sleeveless dresses on the
streets of London.

The city did not look much like the capital of a nation
at war. There were signs, of course; and Henry Faber, cy-
cling from Waterloo Station toward Highgate, noted them:
piles of sandbags outside important public buildings, Anderson shelters in suburban gardens, propaganda posters
about evacuation and Air Raid Precautions. Faber watched
such things—he was considerably more observant than the
average railway clerk. He saw crowds of children in the
parks, and concluded that evacuation had been a failure. He
marked the number of motor cars on the road, despite petrol
rationing; and he read about the new models announced by
the motor manufacturers. He knew the significance of
night-shift workers pouring into factories where, only

3

months previously, there had been hardly enough work for the day shift. Most of all, he monitored the movement of troops around Britain's railway network; all the paperwork passed through his office. One could learn a lot from that paperwork. Today, for example, he had rubber-stamped a batch of forms that led him to believe that a new Expeditionary Force was being gathered. He was fairly sure that it would have a complement of about 100,000 men, and that it was for Finland.

There were signs, yes; but there was something jokey about it all. Radio shows satirized the red tape of wartime regulations, there was community singing in the air raid shelters, and fashionable women carried their gas masks in couturier-designed containers. They talked about the Bore War. It was at once larger-than-life and trivial, like a moving picture show. All the air raid warnings, without exception, had been false alarms.

Faber had a different point of view—but then, he was a different kind of person.

He steered his cycle into Archway Road and leaned forward a little to take the uphill slope, his long legs pumping as tirelessly as the pistons of a railway engine. He was very fit for his age, which was thirty-nine, although he lied about it; he lied about most things, as a safety precaution.

He began to perspire as he climbed the hill into Highgate. The building in which he lived was one of the highest in London, which was why he chose to live there. It was a Victorian brick house at one end of a terrace of six. The houses were high, narrow and dark, like the minds of the men for whom they had been built. Each had three stories plus a basement with a servants' entrance—the English middle class of the nineteenth century insisted on a servants' entrance, even if they had no servants. Faber was a cynic about the English.

Number Six had been owned by Mr. Harold Garden, of Garden's Tea and Coffee, a small company that went broke in the Depression. Having lived by the principle that insolvency is a mortal sin, the bankrupt Mr. Garden had no option but to die. The house was all he bequeathed to his widow, who was then obliged to take in boarders. She enjoyed being a landlady, although the etiquette of her social circle demanded that she pretend to be a little ashamed of it. Faber had a room on the top floor with a dormer window. He lived there from Monday to Friday, and told Mrs. Garden that he spent weekends with his mother in Erith. In fact, he had another landlady in Blackheath who called him Mr. Baker and believed he was a traveling salesman for a stationery manufacturer and spent all week on the road.

He wheeled his cycle up the garden path under the disapproving frown of the tall front-room windows. He put it in the shed and padlocked it to the lawn mower—it was against the law to leave a vehicle unlocked. The seed potatoes in boxes all around the shed were sprouting. Mrs. Garden had turned her flower beds over to vegetables for the war effort.

Faber entered the house, hung his hat on the hall-stand, washed his hands and went in to tea.

Three of the other lodgers were already eating: a pimply boy from Yorkshire who was trying to get into the Army; a confectionery salesman with receding sandy hair; and a retired naval officer who, Faber was convinced, was a degenerate. Faber nodded to them and sat down.

The salesman was telling a joke. "So the Squadron Leader says, 'You're back early!' and the pilot turns round and says, 'Yes, I dropped my leaflets in bundles, wasn't that right?' So the Squadron Leader says, 'Good God! You might've hurt somebody!' "

The naval officer cackled and Faber smiled. Mrs. Garden came in with a teapot. "Good evening, Mr. Faber. We started without you—I hope you don't mind."

Faber spread margarine thinly on a slice of wholemeal bread, and momentarily yearned for a fat sausage. "Your seed potatoes are ready to plant," he told her.

Faber hurried through his tea. The others were arguing

over whether Chamberlain should be sacked and replaced
by Churchill. Mrs. Garden kept voicing opinions, then
looking at Faber for a reaction. She was a blowsy woman,
a little overweight. About Faber's age, she wore the clothes
of a woman of thirty, and he guessed she wanted another
husband. He kept out of the discussion.

Mrs. Garden turned on the radio. It hummed for a while,
then an announcer said: "This is the BBC Home Service.
It's That Man Again!"

Faber had heard the show. It regularly featured a German
spy called Funf. He excused himself and went up to his
room.

Mrs. Garden was left alone after "It's That Man Again";
the naval officer went to the pub with the salesman, and
the boy from Yorkshire, who was religious, went to a
prayer meeting. She sat in the parlor with a small glass of
gin, looking at the blackout curtains and thinking about Mr.
Faber. She wished he wouldn't spend so much time in his
room. She needed company, and he was the kind of company she needed.

Such thoughts made her feel guilty. To assuage the guilt,
she thought of Mr. Garden. Her memories were familiar
but blurred, like an old print of a movie with worn sprocket
holes and an indistinct soundtrack; so that, although she
could easily remember what it was like to have him here
in the room with her, it was difficult to imagine his face or
the clothes he might be wearing or the comment he would
make on the day's war news. He had been a small, dapper
man, successful in business when he was lucky and unsuc-
cessful when he was not, undemonstrative in public and
insatiably affectionate in bed. She had loved him a lot.
There would be many women in her position if this war
ever got going properly. She poured another drink.

Mr. Faber was a quiet one—that was the trouble. He
didn't seem to have any vices. He didn't smoke, she had
never smelled drink on his breath, and he spent every eve-

ning in his room, listening to classical music on his radio. He read a lot of newspapers and went for long walks. She suspected he was quite clever, despite his humble job: his contributions to the conversation in the dining room were always a shade more thoughtful than anyone else's. He surely could get a better job if he tried. He seemed not to give himself the chance he deserved.

It was the same with his appearance. He was a fine figure of a man: tall, quite heavy around the neck and shoulders, not a bit fat, with long legs. And he had a strong face, with a high forehead and a long jaw and bright blue eyes; not pretty like a film star, but the kind of face that appealed to a woman. Except for the mouth—that was small and thin, and she could imagine him being cruel. Mr. Garden had been incapable of cruelty.

And yet at first sight he was not the kind of a man a woman would look at twice. The trousers of his old worn suit were never pressed—she would have done that for him, and gladly, but he never asked—and he always wore a shabby raincoat and a flat docker's cap. He had no moustache, and his hair was trimmed short every fortnight. It was as if he wanted to look like a nonentity.

He needed a woman, there was no doubt of that. She wondered for a moment whether he might be what people called effeminate, but she dismissed the idea quickly. He needed a wife to smarten him up and give him ambition. She needed a man to keep her company and for—well—love.

Yet he never made a move. Sometimes she could scream with frustration. She was sure she was attractive. She looked in a mirror as she poured another gin. She had a nice face and fair curly hair, and there was something for a man to get hold of. . . . She giggled at that thought. She must be getting tiddly.

She sipped her drink and considered whether *she* ought to make the first move. Mr. Faber was obviously shy— chronically shy. He wasn't sexless—she could tell by the look in his eyes on the two occasions he had seen her in her nightdress. Perhaps she could overcome his shyness by being brazen. What did she have to lose? She tried imagining the worst, just to see what it felt like. Suppose he rejected her. Well, it would be embarrassing—even humiliating. It would be a blow to her pride. But nobody else need know it had happened. He would just have to leave.

The thought of rejection had put her off the whole idea. She got to her feet slowly, thinking: I'm just not the brazen type. It was bedtime. If she had one more gin in bed she would be able to sleep. She took the bottle upstairs.

Her bedroom was below Mr. Faber's, and she could hear violin music from his radio as she undressed. She put on a new nightdress—pink, with an embroidered neckline, and no one to see it!—and made her last drink. She wondered what Mr. Faber looked like undressed. He would have a flat stomach and hairs on his nipples, and you would be able to see his ribs because he was slim. He probably had a small bottom. She giggled again: thinking, I'm a disgrace.

She took her drink to bed and picked up her book, but it was too much effort to focus on the print. Besides, she was bored with vicarious romance. Stories about dangerous love affairs were fine when you yourself had a perfectly safe love affair with your husband, but a woman needed more than Barbara Cartland. She sipped her gin and wished Mr. Faber would turn the radio off. It was like trying to sleep at a tea dance!

She could, of course, ask him to turn it off. She looked at her bedside clock; it was past ten. She could put on her dressing gown, which matched the nightdress, and just comb her hair a little, then step into her slippers—quite dainty, with a pattern of roses—and just pop up the stairs to the next landing, and just, well, tap on his door. He would open it, perhaps wearing his trousers and undershirt, and then he would *look* at her the way he had *looked* when he saw her in her nightdress on the way to the bathroom. . . .

"Silly old fool," she said to herself aloud. "You're just making excuses to go up there."

And then she wondered why she needed excuses. She was a grownup, and it was her house, and in ten years she had not met another man who was just right for her, and what the *hell*, she needed to feel someone strong and hard and hairy on top of her, squeezing her breasts and panting in her ear and parting her thighs with his broad flat hands, for tomorrow the gas bombs might come over from Germany and they would all die choking and gasping and poisoned and she would have lost her last chance.

So she drained her glass and got out of bed and put on her dressing gown, and just combed her hair a little and stepped into her slippers, and picked up her bunch of keys in case he had locked the door and couldn't hear her knock above the sound of the radio.

There was nobody on the landing. She found the stairs in the darkness. She intended to step over the stair that creaked, but she stumbled on the loose carpet and trod on it heavily; but it seemed that nobody heard, so she went on up and tapped on the door at the top. She tried it gently. It was locked.

The radio was turned down and Mr. Faber called out, "Yes?"

He was well-spoken; not cockney or foreign—not anything, really, just a pleasantly neutral voice.

She said, "Can I have a word with you?"

He seemed to hesitate, then he said: "I'm undressed."

"So am I," she giggled, and she opened the door with her duplicate key.

He was standing in front of the radio with some kind of screwdriver in his hand. He wore his trousers and *no* undershirt. His face was white and he looked scared to death.

She stepped inside and closed the door behind her, not knowing what to say. Suddenly she remembered a line from an American film, and she said, "Would you buy a lonely girl a drink?" It was silly, really, because she knew he had no drink in his room and she certainly wasn't dressed to go out; but it sounded vampish.

It seemed to have the desired effect. Without speaking, he came slowly toward her. He *did* have hair on his nipples. She took a step forward, and then his arms went around her and she closed her eyes and turned up her face, and he kissed her, and she moved slightly in his arms, and then there was a terrible, awful, unbearable sharp pain in her back and she opened her mouth to scream.

He had heard her stumble on the stairs. If she'd waited another minute he would have had the radio transmitter back in its case and the code books in the drawer and there would have been no need for her to die. But before he could conceal the evidence he had heard her key in the lock, and when she opened the door the stiletto had been in his hand.

Because she moved slightly in his arms, Faber missed her heart with the first jab of the weapon, and he had to thrust his fingers down her throat to stop her crying out. He jabbed again, but she moved again and the blade struck a rib and merely slashed her superficially. Then the blood was spurting and he knew it would not be a clean kill; it never was when you missed the first stroke.

She was wriggling too much to be killed with a jab now. Keeping his fingers in her mouth, he gripped her jaw with his thumb and pushed her back against the door. Her head hit the woodwork with a loud bump, and he wished he had not turned the radio down, but how could he have expected this?

He hesitated before killing her because it would be much better if she died on the bed—better for the cover-up that was already taking shape in his mind—but he could not be sure of getting her that far in silence. He tightened his hold on her jaw, kept her head still by jamming it against the door, and brought the stiletto around in a wide, slashing arc that ripped away most of her throat, for the stiletto was not a slashing knife and the throat was not Faber's favored target.

He jumped back to avoid the first horrible gush of blood, then stepped forward again to catch her before she hit the floor. He dragged her to the bed, trying not to look at her neck, and laid her down.

He had killed before, so he expected the reaction—it always came as soon as he felt safe. He went over to the sink in the corner of the room and waited for it. He could see his face in the little shaving mirror. He was white and his eyes were staring. He looked at himself and thought, killer. Then he threw up.

When that was over he felt better. He could go to work now. He knew what he had to do, the details had come to him even while he was killing her.

He washed his face, brushed his teeth and cleaned the washbasin. Then he sat down at the table beside his radio. He looked at his notebook, found his place and began tapping the key. It was a long message, about the mustering of an army for Finland, and he had been halfway through when he was interrupted. It was written down in cipher on the pad. When he had completed it he signed off with "Regards to Willi."

The transmitter packed away neatly into a specially designed suitcase. Faber put the rest of his possessions into a second case. He took off his trousers and sponged the bloodstains, then washed himself all over.

At last he looked at the corpse.

He was able to be cold about her now. It was wartime; they were enemies; if he had not killed her she would have caused his death. She had been a threat, and all he felt now was relief that the threat had been nullified. She should not have frightened him.

Nevertheless, his last task was distasteful. He opened her robe and lifted her nightdress, pulling it up around her waist. She was wearing knickers. He tore them, so that the hair of her pubis was visible. Poor woman, she had wanted only to seduce him. But he could not have got her out of the room without her seeing the transmitter, and the British propaganda had made these people alert for spies—ridiculously so. If the Abwehr had as many agents as the newspapers made out, the British would have lost the war already.

He stepped back and looked at her with his head on one side. There was something wrong. He tried to think like a sex maniac. If I were crazed with lust for a woman like Una Garden, and I killed just so that I could have my way with her, what would I then do?

Of course, that kind of lunatic would want to look at her breasts. Faber leaned over the body, gripped the neckline of the nightdress, and ripped it to the waist. Her large breasts sagged sideways.

The police doctor would soon discover that she had not been raped, but Faber did not think that mattered. He had taken a criminology course at Heidelberg, and he knew that many sexual assaults·were not consummated. Besides, he could not have carried the deception that far, not even for the Fatherland. He was not in the SS. Some of *them* would queue up to rape the corpse. . . . He put the thought out of his mind.

He washed his hands again and got dressed. It was almost midnight. He would wait an hour before leaving, it would be safer later.

He sat down to think about how he had gone wrong.

There was no question that he had made a mistake. If his cover were perfect, he would be totally secure. If he were totally secure no one could discover his secret. Mrs. Garden had discovered his secret—or rather, she would have if she had lived a few seconds longer—therefore he had not been totally secure, therefore his cover was not perfect, therefore he had made a mistake.

He should have put a bolt on the door. Better to be thought chronically shy than to have landladies with duplicate keys sneaking in in their nightclothes.

That was the surface error. The deep flaw was that he was too eligible to be a bachelor. He thought this with irritation, not conceit. He knew that he was a pleasant, attractive man and that there was no apparent reason why he should be single. He turned his mind to thinking up a cover that would explain this without inviting advances from the Mrs. Gardens of this world.

He ought to be able to find inspiration in his real personality. Why *was* he single? He stirred uneasily—he did not like mirrors. The answer was simple. He was single because of his profession. If there were deeper reasons, he did not want to know them.

He would have to spend tonight in the open. Highgate Wood would do. In the morning he would take his suitcases to a railway station checkroom, then tomorrow evening he would go to his room in Blackheath.

He would shift to his second identity. He had little fear of being caught by the police. The commercial traveler who occupied the room at Blackheath on weekends looked rather different from the railway clerk who had killed his landlady. The Blackheath persona was expansive, vulgar and flashy. He wore loud ties, bought rounds of drinks, and combed his hair differently. The police would circulate a description of a shabby little pervert who would not say boo to a goose until he was inflamed with lust, and no one would look twice at the handsome salesman in the striped suit who was obviously the type that was more or less permanently inflamed with lust and did not have to kill women to get them to show him their breasts.

He would have to set up another identity—he always kept at least two. He needed a new job, fresh papers—passport, identity card, ration book, birth certificate. It was all so *risky*. Damn Mrs. Garden. Why couldn't she have drunk herself asleep as usual?

It was one o'clock. Faber took a last look around the room. He was not concerned about leaving clues—his fingerprints were obviously all over the house, and there would be no doubt in anyone's mind about who was the murderer. Nor did he feel any sentiment about leaving the place that had been his home for two years; he had never thought of it as home. He had never thought of anywhere as home.

He would always think of this as the place where he had learned to put a bolt on a door.

He turned out the light, picked up his cases, and went down the stairs and out of the door into the night.

2

HENRY II WAS A REMARKABLE KING. IN AN AGE when the term "flying visit" had not yet been coined, he flitted between England and France with such rapidity that he was credited with magical powers; a rumor that, understandably, he did nothing to suppress. In 1173—either the June or the September, depending upon which secondary source one favors—he arrived in England and left for France again so quickly that no contemporary writer ever found out about it. Later historians discovered the record of his expenditure in the Pipe Rolls. At the time his kingdom was under attack by his sons at its northern and southern extremes—the Scottish border and the South of France. But what, precisely, was the purpose of his visit? Whom did he see? Why was it secret, when the myth of his magical speed was worth an army? What did he accomplish?

This was the problem that taxed Percival Godliman in the summer of 1940, when Hitler's armies swept across the French cornfields like a scythe and the British poured out of the Dunkirk bottleneck in bloody disarray.

Professor Godliman knew more about the Middle Ages than any man alive. His book on the Black Death had upended every convention of medievalism; it had also been a best-seller and published as a Penguin Book. With that behind him he had turned to a slightly earlier and even more intractable period.

At 12:30 on a splendid June day in London, a secretary

15

found Godliman hunched over an illuminated manuscript, laboriously translating its medieval Latin, making notes in his own even less legible handwriting. The secretary, who was planning to eat her lunch in the garden of Gordon Square, did not like the manuscript room because it smelled dead. You needed so many keys to get in there, it might as well have been a tomb.

Godliman stood at a lectern, perched on one leg like a bird, his face lit bleakly by a spotlight above—he might have been the ghost of the monk who wrote the book, standing a cold vigil over his precious chronicle. The girl cleared her throat and waited for him to notice her. She saw a short man in his fifties, with round shoulders and weak eyesight, wearing a tweed suit. She knew he could be perfectly sensible once you dragged him out of the Middle Ages. She coughed again and said, "Professor Godliman?"

He looked up, and when he saw her he smiled, and then he did not look like a ghost, more like someone's dotty father. "Hello!" he said, in an astonished tone, as if he had just met his next-door neighbor in the middle of the Sahara Desert.

"You asked me to remind you that you have lunch at the Savoy with Colonel Terry."

"Oh, yes." He took his watch out of his waistcoat pocket and peered at it. "If I'm going to walk it, I'd better leave now."

She nodded. "I brought your gas mask."

"You are thoughtful!" He smiled again, and she decided he looked quite nice. He took the mask from her and said, "Do I need my coat?"

"You didn't wear one this morning. It's quite warm. Shall I lock up after you?"

"Thank you, thank you." He jammed his notebook into his jacket pocket and went out.

The secretary looked around, shivered, and followed him.

*   *   *

Colonel Andrew Terry was a red-faced Scot, pauper-thin from a lifetime of heavy smoking, with sparse dark-blond hair thickly brilliantined. Godliman found him at a corner table in the Savoy Grill, wearing civilian clothes. There were three cigarette stubs in the ashtray. He stood up to shake hands.

Godliman said, "Morning, Uncle Andrew." Terry was his mother's baby brother.

"How are you, Percy?"

"I'm writing a book about the Plantagenets." Godliman sat down.

"Are your manuscripts still in London? I'm surprised."

"Why?"

Terry lit another cigarette. "Move them to the country in case of bombing."

"Should I?"

"Half the National Gallery has been shoved into a bloody big hole in the ground somewhere up in Wales. Young Kenneth Clark is quicker off the mark than you. Might be sensible to take yourself off out of it too, while you're about it. I don't suppose you've many students left."

"That's true." Godliman took a menu from a waiter and said, "I don't want a drink."

Terry did not look at his menu. "Seriously, Percy, why are you still in town?"

Godliman's eyes seemed to clear, like the image on a screen when the projector is focused, as if he had to think for the first time since he walked in. "It's all right for children to leave, and national institutions like Bertrand Russell. But for me—well, it's a bit like running away and letting other people fight for you. I realize that's not a strictly logical argument. It's a matter of sentiment, not logic."

Terry smiled the smile of one whose expectations have been fulfilled. But he dropped the subject and looked at the menu. After a moment he said, "Good God. *Le Lord Woolton Pie.*"

Godliman grinned. "I'm sure it's still just potatoes and vegetables."

When they had ordered, Terry said, "What do you think of our new Prime Minister?"

"The man's an ass. But then, Hitler's a fool, and look how well he's doing. You?"

"We can live with Winston. At least he's bellicose."

Godliman raised his eyebrows. " 'We'? Are you back in the game?"

"I never really left it, you know."

"But you said—"

"Percy. Can't you think of a department whose staff all say they don't work for the Army?"

"Well, I'm damned. All this time . . ."

Their first course came, and they started a bottle of white Bordeaux. Godliman ate potted salmon and looked pensive.

Eventually Terry said, "Thinking about the last lot?"

Godliman nodded. "Young days, you know. Terrible time." But his tone was almost wistful.

"This war isn't the same at all. My chaps don't go behind enemy lines and count bivouacs like you did. Well, they do, but that side of things is much less important this time. Nowadays we just listen to the wireless."

"Don't they broadcast in code?"

Terry shrugged. "Codes can be broken. Candidly, we get to know just about everything we need these days."

Godliman glanced around, but there was no one within earshot, and it was hardly for him to tell Terry that careless talk costs lives.

Terry went on, "In fact my job is to make sure *they* don't have the information they need about *us*."

They both had chicken pie to follow. There was no beef on the menu. Godliman fell silent, but Terry talked on.

"Canaris is a funny chap, you know. Admiral Wilhelm Canaris, head of the Abwehr. I met him before this lot started. Likes England. My guess is he's none too fond of Hitler. Anyway, we know he's been told to mount a major intelligence operation against us, in preparation for the invasion—but he's not doing much. We arrested their best man in England the day after war broke out. He's in Wandsworth prison now. Useless people, Canaris's spies. Old ladies in boarding-houses, mad Fascists, petty criminals—"

Godliman said, "Look here, old boy, this is too much." He trembled slightly with a mixture of anger and incomprehension. "All this stuff is secret. I don't want to know!"

Terry was unperturbed. "Would you like something else?" he offered. "I'm having chocolate ice cream."

Godliman stood up. "I don't think so. I'm going to go back to my work, if you don't mind."

Terry looked up at him coolly. "The world can wait for your reappraisal of the Plantagenets, Percy. There's a war on, dear boy. I want you to work for me."

Godliman stared down at him for a long moment. "What on earth would I do?"

Terry smiled wolfishly. "Catch spies."

Walking back to the college, Godliman felt depressed despite the weather. He would accept Colonel Terry's offer, no doubt about that. His country was at war; it was a just war; and if he was too old to fight, he was still young enough to help.

But the thought of leaving his work—and for how many years?—depressed him. He loved history and he had been totally absorbed in medieval England since the death of his wife ten years ago. He liked the unraveling of mysteries, the discovery of faint clues, the resolution of contradictions, the unmasking of lies and propaganda and myth. His new book would be the best on its subject written in the last hundred years, and there would not be one to equal it for another century. It had ruled his life for so long that the thought of abandoning it was almost unreal, as difficult to digest as the discovery that one is an orphan and no relation at all to the people one has always called Mother and Father.

An air raid warning stridently interrupted his thoughts. He contemplated ignoring it—so many people did now, and he was only ten minutes' walk from the college. But he had no real reason to return to his study—he knew he would do no more work today. So he hurried into a tube station and joined the solid mass of Londoners crowding down the staircases and on to the grimy platform. He stood close to the wall, staring at a Bovril poster, and thought, But it's not just the things I'm leaving behind.

Going back into the game depressed him, too. There were some things he liked about it: the importance of *little* things, the value of simply being clever, the meticulousness, the guesswork. But he hated the blackmail, the deceit, the desperation, and the way one always stabbed the enemy in the back.

The platform was becoming more crowded. Godliman sat down while there was still room, and found himself leaning against a man in a bus driver's uniform. The man smiled and said, "Oh to be in England, now that summer's here. Know who said that?"

"Now that April's there," Godliman corrected him. "It was Browning."

"I heard it was Adolf Hitler," the driver said. A woman next to him squealed with laughter and he turned his attention to her. "Did you hear what the evacuee said to the farmer's wife?"

Godliman tuned out and remembered an April when he had longed for England, crouching on a high branch of a plane tree, peering through a cold mist across a French valley behind the German lines. He could see nothing but vague dark shapes, even through his telescope, and he was about to slide down and walk a mile or so farther when three German soldiers came from nowhere to sit around the base of the tree and smoke. After a while they took out cards and began to play, and young Percival Godliman realized they had found a way of stealing off and were here for the day. He stayed in the tree, hardly moving, until he began to shiver and his muscles knotted with cramp and his bladder felt as if it would burst. Then he took out his revolver and shot the three of them, one after the another, through the tops of their close-cropped heads. And three people, laughing and cursing and gambling their pay, had simply ceased to exist. It was the first time he killed, and all he could think was, Just because I had to pee.

Godliman shifted on the cold concrete of the station platform and let the memory fade away. There was a warm wind from the tunnel and a train came in. The people who got off found spaces and settled to wait. Godliman listened to the voices.

"Did you hear Churchill on the wireless? We was listening-in at the Duke of Wellington. Old Jack Thornton cried. Silly old bugger . . ."

"Haven't had fillet steak on the menu for so long I've forgotten the bally taste . . . wine committee saw the war coming and brought in twenty thousand dozen, thank God . . ."

"Yes, a quiet wedding, but what's the point in waiting when you don't know what the next day's going to bring?"

"No, Peter never came back from Dunkirk . . ."

The bus driver offered him a cigarette. Godliman refused, and took out his pipe. Someone started to sing.

> *A blackout warden passing yelled,*
> *"Ma, pull down that blind—*
> *Just look at what you're showing," and we*
> *Shouted, "Never mind." Oh!*
> *Knees up Mother Brown . . .*

The song spread through the crowd until everyone was singing. Godliman joined in, knowing that this was a nation losing a war and singing to hide to its fear, as a man will whistle past the graveyard at night; knowing that the sudden affection he felt for London and Londoners was an ephemeral sentiment, akin to mob hysteria; mistrusting the voice inside him that said "This, this is what the war is about, this is what makes it worth fighting"; knowing but not caring, because for the first time in so many years he was feeling the sheer physical thrill of comradeship and he liked it.

When the all-clear sounded they went up the staircase and into the street, and Godliman found a phone box and called Colonel Terry to ask how soon he could start.

3

FABER . . . GODLIMAN . . . TWO-THIRDS OF A TRIAN-
gle that one day would be crucially completed by the
principals, David and Lucy, of a ceremony proceeding
at this moment in a small country church. It was old and
very beautiful. A dry-stone wall enclosed a graveyard
where wildflowers grew. The church itself had been there—
well, bits of it had—the last time Britain was invaded, almost a millennium ago. The north wall of the nave, several
feet thick and pierced with only two tiny windows, could
remember that last invasion; it had been built when
churches were places of physical as well as spiritual sanc-
tuary, and the little round-headed windows were better for
shooting arrows out of than for letting the Lord's sunshine
in. Indeed, the Local Defense Volunteers had detailed plans
for using the church if and when the current bunch of European thugs crossed the Channel.

But no jackboots sounded in the tiled choir in this August
of 1940; not yet. The sun glowed through stained glass
windows that had survived Cromwell's iconoclasts and
Henry VIII's greed, and the roof resounded to the notes of
an organ that had yet to yield to woodworm and dry rot.

It was a lovely wedding. Lucy wore white, of course,
and her five sisters were bridesmaids in apricot dresses.
David wore the Mess Uniform of a Flying Officer in the
Royal Air Force, all crisp and new for it was the first time
he had put it on. They sang Psalm 23, The Lord Is My
Shepherd, to the tune *Crimond*.

Lucy's father looked proud, as a man will on the day his eldest and most beautiful daughter marries a fine boy in a uniform. He was a farmer, but it was a long time since he had sat on a tractor; he rented out his arable land and used the rest to raise racehorses, although this winter of course his pasture would go under the plough and potatoes would be planted. Although he was really more gentleman than farmer, he nevertheless had the open-air skin, the deep chest, and the big stubby hands of agricultural people. Most of the men on that side of the church bore him a resemblance: barrel-chested men, with weathered red faces, those not in tail coats favoring tweed suits and stout shoes.

The bridesmaids had something of that look, too; they were country girls. But the bride was like her mother. Her hair was a dark, dark red, long and thick and shining and glorious, and she had wide-apart amber eyes and an oval face; and when she looked at the vicar with that clear, direct gaze and said, "I will" in that firm, clear voice, the vicar was startled and thought "By God she means it!" which was an odd thought for a vicar to have in the middle of a wedding.

The family on the other side of the nave had a certain look about them, too. David's father was a lawyer—his permanent frown was a professional affectation and concealed a sunny nature. (He had been a Major in the Army in the last war, and thought all this business about the RAF and war in the air was a fad that would soon pass.) But nobody looked like him, not even his son who stood now at the altar promising to love his wife until death, which might not be far away, God forbid. No, they all looked like David's mother, who sat beside her husband now, with almost-black hair and dark skin and long, slender limbs.

David was the tallest of the lot. He had broken high-jump records last year at Cambridge University. He was rather too good-looking for a man—his face would have been feminine were it not for the dark, ineradicable shadow of a heavy beard. He shaved twice a day. He had long eyelashes, and he looked intelligent, which he was, and sensitive.

The whole thing was idyllic: two happy, handsome people, children of solid, comfortably off, backbone-of-England-type families getting married in a country church in the finest summer weather Britain can offer.

When they were pronounced man and wife both the mothers were dry-eyed, and both the fathers cried.

Kissing the bride was a barbarous custom, Lucy thought, as yet another middle-aged pair of champagne-wet lips smeared her cheek. It was probably descended from even more barbarous customs in the Dark Ages, when every man in the tribe was allowed to—well, anyway, it was time we got properly civilized and dropped the whole business.

She had known she would not like this part of the wedding. She liked champagne, but she was not crazy about chicken drumsticks or dollops of caviar on squares of cold toast, and as for the speeches and the photographs and the honeymoon jokes, well . . . But it could have been worse. If it had been peacetime Father would have hired the Albert Hall.

So far nine people had said, "May all your troubles be little ones," and one person, with scarcely more originality, had said, "I want to see more than a fence running around your garden." Lucy had shaken countless hands and pretended not to hear remarks like "I wouldn't mind being in David's pajamas tonight." David had made a speech in which he thanked Lucy's parents for giving him their daughter, and Lucy's father actually said that he was not losing a daughter but gaining a son. It was all hopelessly gaga, but one did it for one's parents.

A distant uncle loomed up from the direction of the bar, swaying slightly, and Lucy repressed a shudder. She introduced him to her husband. "David, this is Uncle Norman."

Uncle Norman pumped David's bony hand. "Well, m'boy, when do you take up your commission?"

"Tomorrow, sir."

"What, no honeymoon?"

"Just twenty-four hours."

"But you've only just finished your training, so I gather."

"Yes, but I could fly before, you know. I learned at Cambridge. Besides, with all this going on they can't spare pilots. I expect I shall be in the air tomorrow."

Lucy said quietly, "David, don't," but Uncle Norman persevered.

"What'll you fly?" Uncle Norman asked with schoolboy enthusiasm.

"Spitfire. I saw her yesterday. She's a lovely kite." David had already fallen into the RAF slang—kites and crates and the drink and bandits at two o'clock. "She's got eight guns, she does three hundred and fifty knots, and she'll turn around in a shoebox."

"Marvelous, marvelous. You boys are certainly knocking the stuffing out of the Luftwaffe, what?"

"We got sixty yesterday for eleven of our own," David said, as proudly as if he had shot them all down himself. "The day before, when they had a go at Yorkshire, we sent the lot back to Norway with their tails between their legs—and we didn't lose a single kite!"

Uncle Norman gripped David's shoulder with tipsy fervor. "Never," he quoted pompously, "was so much owed by so many to so few. Churchill said that the other day."

David tried a modest grin. "He must have been talking about the mess bills."

Lucy hated the way they trivialized bloodshed and destruction. She said: "David, we should go and change now."

They went in separate cars to Lucy's home. Her mother helped her out of the wedding dress and said: "Now, my dear, I don't quite know what you're expecting tonight, but you ought to know—"

"Oh, mother, this *is* 1940, you know!"

Her mother colored slightly. "Very well, dear," she said

mildly. "But if there is anything you want to talk about, later on . . ."

It occurred to Lucy that to say things like this cost her mother considerable effort, and she regretted her sharp reply. "Thank you," she said. She touched her mother's hand. "I will."

"I'll leave you to it, then. Call me if you want anything." She kissed Lucy's cheek and went out.

Lucy sat at the dressing table in her slip and began to brush her hair. She knew exactly what to expect tonight. She felt a faint glow of pleasure as she remembered.

It happened in June, a year after they had met at the Glad Rag Ball. They were seeing each other every week by this time, and David had spent part of the Easter vacation with Lucy's people. Mother and Father approved of him—he was handsome, clever and gentlemanly, and he came from precisely the same stratum of society as they did. Father thought he was a shade too opinionated, but Mother said the landed gentry had been saying that about undergraduates for six hundred years, and *she* thought David would be kind to his wife, which was the most important thing in the long run. So in June Lucy went to David's family home for a weekend.

The place was a Victorian copy of an eighteenth-century grange, a square-shaped house with nine bedrooms and a terrace with a vista. What impressed Lucy about it was the realization that the people who planted the garden must have known they would be long dead before it reached maturity. The atmosphere was very easy, and the two of them drank beer on the terrace in the afternoon sunshine. That was when David told her that he had been accepted for officer training in the RAF, along with four pals from the university flying club. He wanted to be a fighter pilot.

"I can fly all right," he said, "and they'll need people once this war gets going—they say it'll be won and lost in the air, this time."

"Aren't you afraid?" she said quietly.

"Not a bit," he said. Then he looked at her and said, "Yes, I am."

She thought he was very brave, and held his hand.

A little later they put on swimming suits and went down to the lake. The water was clear and cool, but the sun was still strong and the air was warm as they splashed about gleefully.

"Are you a good swimmer?" he asked her.

"Better than you!"

"All right. Race you to the island."

She shaded her eyes to look into the sun. She held the pose for a minute, pretending she did not know how desirable she was in her wet swimsuit with her arms raised and her shoulders back. The island was a small patch of bushes and trees about three hundred yards away, in the center of the lake.

She dropped her hands, shouted, "Go!" and struck out in a fast crawl.

David won, of course, with his enormously long arms and legs. Lucy found herself in difficulty when she was still fifty yards from the island. She switched to breaststroke, but she was too exhausted even for that, and she had to roll over on to her back and float. David, who was already sitting on the bank blowing like a walrus, slipped back into the water and swam to meet her. He got behind her, held her beneath the arms in the correct lifesaving position, and pulled her slowly to shore. His hands were just below her breasts.

"I'm enjoying this," he said, and she giggled despite her breathlessness.

A few moments later he said, "I suppose I might as well tell you."

"What?" she panted.

"The lake is only four feet deep."

"You . . . !" She wriggled out of his arms, spluttering and laughing, and found her footing.

He took her hand and led her out of the water and

through the trees. He pointed to an old wooden rowboat rotting upside-down beneath a hawthorn. "When I was a boy I used to row out here in that, with one of Papa's pipes, a box of matches and a pinch of St. Bruno in a twist of paper. This is where I used to smoke it."

They were in a clearing, completely surrounded by bushes. The turf underfoot was clean and springy. Lucy flopped on the ground.

"We'll swim back slowly," David said.

"Let's not even talk about it just yet," she replied.

He sat beside her and kissed her, then pushed her gently backwards until she was lying down. He stroked her hip and kissed her throat, and soon she stopped shivering. When he laid his hand gently, nervously, on the soft mound between her legs, she arched upwards, willing him to press harder. She pulled his face to hers and kissed him open-mouthed and wetly. His hands went to the straps of her swimsuit, and he pulled them down over her shoulders. She said, "No."

He buried his face between her breasts. "Lucy, please."

"No."

He looked at her. "It might be my last chance."

She rolled away from him and stood up. Then, because of the war, and because of the pleading look on his flushed young face, and because of the glow inside her which would not go away, she took off her costume with one swift movement and removed her bathing cap so that her dark-red hair shook out over her shoulders. She knelt in front of him, taking his face in her hands and guiding his lips to her breast.

She lost her virginity painlessly, enthusiastically, and only a little too quickly.

The spice of guilt made the memory more pleasant, not less. Even if it had been a well-planned seduction then she had been a willing, not to say eager, victim, especially at the end.

She began to dress in her going-away outfit. She had startled him a couple of times that afternoon on the island: once when she wanted him to kiss her breasts, and again when she had guided him inside her with her hands. Apparently such things did not happen in the books he read. Like most of her friends, Lucy read D. H. Lawrence for information about sex. She believed in his choreography and mistrusted the sound effects—the things his people did to one another sounded nice, but not that nice; she was not expecting trumpets and thunderstorms and the clash of cymbals at her sexual awakening.

David was a little more ignorant than she, but he was gentle, and he took pleasure in her pleasure, and she was sure that was the important thing.

They had done it only once since the first time. Exactly a week before their wedding they had made love again, and it caused their first row.

This time it was at her parents' house, in the morning after everyone else had left. He came to her room in his robe and got into bed with her. She almost changed her mind about Lawrence's trumpets and cymbals. David got out of bed immediately afterward.

"Don't go," she said.

"Somebody might come in."

"I'll chance it. Come back to bed." She was warm and drowsy and comfortable, and she wanted him beside her.

He put on his robe. "It makes me nervous."

"You weren't nervous five minutes ago." She reached for him. "Lie with me. I want to get to know your body."

Her directness obviously embarrassed him, and he turned away.

She flounced out of bed, her lovely breasts heaving. "You're making me feel cheap!" She sat on the edge of the bed and burst into tears.

David put his arms around her and said: "I'm sorry, sorry, sorry. You're the first for me, too, and I don't know what to expect, and I feel confused . . . I mean, nobody tells you anything about this, do they?"

She snuffled and shook her head in agreement, and it occurred to her that what was *really* unnerving him was the knowledge that in eight days' time he had to take off in a flimsy aircraft and fight for his life above the clouds; so she forgave him, and he dried her tears, and they got back into bed. He was very sweet after that. . . .

She was just about ready. She examined herself in a full-length mirror. Her suit was faintly military, with square shoulders and epaulettes, but the blouse beneath it was feminine, for balance. Her hair fell in sausage curls beneath a natty pill-box hat. It would not have been right to go away gorgeously dressed, not this year; but she felt she had achieved the kind of briskly practical, yet attractive, look that was rapidly becoming fashionable.

David was waiting for her in the hall. He kissed her and said, "You look wonderful, Mrs. Rose."

They were driven back to the reception to say good-bye to everyone. They were going to spend the night in London, at Claridge's, then David would drive on to Biggin Hill and Lucy would come home again. She was going to live with her parents—she had the use of a cottage for when David was on leave.

There was another half-hour of handshakes and kisses, then they went out to the car. Some of David's cousins had got at his open-top MG. There were tin cans and an old boot tied to the bumpers with string, the running-boards were awash with confetti, and "Just Married" was scrawled all over the paintwork in bright red lipstick.

They drove away, smiling and waving, the guests filling the street behind them. A mile down the road they stopped and cleaned up the car.

It was dusk when they got going again. David's headlights were fitted with blackout masks, but he drove very fast just the same. Lucy felt very happy.

David said, "There's a bottle of bubbly in the glove compartment."

Lucy opened the compartment and found the champagne and two glasses carefully wrapped in tissue paper. It was still quite cold. The cork came out with a loud pop and shot off into the night. David lit a cigarette while Lucy poured the wine.

"We're going to be late for supper," he said.

"Who cares?" She handed him a glass.

She was too tired to drink, really. She became sleepy. The car seemed to be going terribly fast. She let David have most of the champagne. He began to whistle *St. Louis Blues*.

Driving through England in the blackout was a weird experience. One missed lights that one hadn't realized were there before the war: lights in cottage porches and farmhouse windows, lights on cathedral spires and inn signs, and—most of all—the luminous glow, low in the distant sky, of the thousand lights of a nearby town. Even if one had been able to see, there were no signposts to look at; they had been removed to confuse the German parachutists who were expected any day. (Just a few days ago in the Midlands, farmers had found parachutes, radios and maps, but since there were no footprints leading away from the objects, it had been concluded that no men had landed, and the whole thing was a feeble Nazi attempt to panic the population.) Anyway, David knew the way to London.

They climbed a long hill. The little sports car took it nimbly. Lucy gazed through half-closed eyes at the blackness ahead. The downside of the hill was steep and winding. Lucy heard the distant roar of an approaching truck.

The MG's tires squealed as David raced around the bends. "I think you're going too fast," Lucy said mildly.

The back of the car skidded on a left curve. David changed down, afraid to brake in case he skidded again. On either side the hedgerows were dimly picked out by the shaded headlights. There was a sharp right-hand curve, and

David lost the back again. The curve seemed to go on and on forever. The little car slid sideways and turned through 180 degrees, so that it was going backwards, then continued to turn in the same direction.

"David!" Lucy screamed.

The moon came out suddenly, and they saw the truck. It was struggling up the hill at a snail's pace, with thick smoke, made silvery by the moonlight pouring from its snout-shaped top. Lucy glimpsed the driver's face, even his cloth cap and his moustache; his mouth was open as he stood on his brakes.

The car was traveling forward again now. There was just room to pass the truck if David could regain control of the car. He heaved the steering wheel over and touched the accelerator. It was a mistake.

The car and the truck collided head-on.

4

FOREIGNERS HAVE SPIES; BRITAIN HAS MILITARY INtelligence. As if that were not euphemism enough, it is abbreviated to MI. In 1940, MI was part of the War Office. It was spreading like crab grass at the time—not surprisingly—and its different sections were known by numbers: MI9 ran the escape routes from prisoner-of-war camps through Occupied Europe to neutral countries; MI8 monitored enemy wireless traffic, and was of more value than six regiments; MI6 sent agents into France.

It was MI5 that Professor Percival Godliman joined in the autumn of 1940. He turned up at the War Office in Whitehall on a cold September morning after a night spent putting out fires all over the East End; the blitz was at its height and he was an auxiliary fireman.

Military Intelligence was run by soldiers in peacetime, when—in Godliman's opinion—espionage made no difference to anything anyhow; but now, he found, it was populated by amateurs, and he was delighted to discover that he knew half the people in MI5. On his first day he met a barrister who was a member of his club, an art historian with whom he had been to college, an archivist from his own university, and his favorite writer of detective stories.

He was shown into Colonel Terry's office at 10 A.M. Terry had been there for several hours; there were two empty cigarette packets in the wastepaper basket.

Godliman said, "Should I call you 'Sir' now?"

"There's not much bull around here, Percy. 'Uncle Andrew' will do fine. Sit down."

All the same, there was a briskness about Terry that had not been present when they had lunch at the Savoy. Godliman noticed that he did not smile, and his attention kept wandering to a pile of unread messages on the desk.

Terry looked at his watch and said, "I'm going to put you in the picture, briefly—finish the lecture I started over lunch."

Godliman smiled. "This time I won't get up on my high horse."

Terry lit another cigarette.

Canaris's spies in Britain were useless people (Terry resumed, as if their conversation had been interrupted five minutes rather than three months ago). Dorothy O'Grady was typical—we caught her cutting military telephone wires on the Isle of Wight. She was writing letters to Portugal in the kind of secret ink you buy in joke shops.

A new wave of spies began in September. Their task was to reconnoiter Britain in preparation for the invasion—to map beaches suitable for landings; fields and roads that could be used by troop-carrying gliders; tank traps and road blocks and barbed-wire obstacles.

They seem to have been badly selected, hastily mustered, inadequately trained and poorly equipped. Typical were the four who came over on the night of 2–3 September: Meier, Kieboom, Pons and Waldberg. Kieboom and Pons landed at dawn near Hythe, and were arrested by Private Tollervey of the Somerset Light Infantry, who came upon them in the sand dunes hacking away at a dirty great *wurst*.

Waldberg actually managed to send a signal to Hamburg: ARRIVED SAFELY. DOCUMENT DESTROYED. ENGLISH PATROL 200 METERS FROM COAST. BEACH WITH BROWN NETS AND RAILWAY SLEEPERS AT A DISTANCE OF 50 METERS. NO MINES. FEW SOL-

DIERS. UNFINISHED BLOCKHOUSE. NEW ROAD. WALDBERG. •

Clearly he did not know where he was, nor did he even have a code name. The quality of his briefing is indicated by the fact that he knew nothing of English licensing laws—he went into a pub at nine o'clock in the morning and asked for a quart of cider.

(Godliman laughed at this, and Terry said: "Wait—it gets funnier.")

The landlord told Waldberg to come back at ten. He could spend the hour looking at the village church, he suggested. Amazingly, Waldberg was back at ten sharp, whereupon two policemen on bicycles arrested him.

("It's like a script for 'It's That Man Again,' " said Godliman.)

Meier was found a few hours later. Eleven more agents were picked up over the next few weeks, most of them within hours of landing on British soil. Almost all of them were destined for the scaffold.

("*Almost* all?" said Godliman. Terry said: "Yes. A couple have been handed over to our section B-1(a). I'll come back to that in a minute.")

Others landed in Eire. One was Ernst Weber-Drohl, a well-known acrobat who had two illegitimate children in Ireland—he had toured music halls there as "The World's Strongest Man." He was arrested by the Garde Siochana, fined three pounds, and turned over to B-1(a).

Another was Hermann Goetz, who parachuted into Ulster instead of Eire by mistake, was robbed by the IRA, swam the Boyne in his fur underwear and eventually swallowed his suicide pill. He had a flashlight marked "Made in Dresden."

("If it's so easy to pick these bunglers up," Terry said, "why are we taking on brainy types like yourself to catch them? Two reasons. One: we've got no way of knowing how many we *haven't* picked up. Two: it's what we do with the ones we don't hang that matters. This is where

B-1(a) comes in. But to explain that I have to go back to 1936.")

Alfred George Owens was an electrical engineer with a company that had a few government contracts. He visited Germany several times during the '30s, and voluntarily gave to the Admiralty odd bits of technical information he picked up there. Eventually Naval Intelligence passed him on to MI6 who began to develop him as an agent. The Abwehr recruited him at about the same time, as MI6 discovered when they intercepted a letter from him to a known German cover address. Clearly he was a man totally without loyalty; he just wanted to be a spy. We called him "Snow"; the Germans called him "Johnny."

In January 1939 Snow got a letter containing (1) instructions for the use of a wireless transmitter and (2) a ticket from the checkroom at Victoria Station.

He was arrested the day after war broke out, and he and his transmitter (which he had picked up, in a suitcase, when he presented the checkroom ticket) were locked up in Wandsworth Prison. He continued to communicate with Hamburg, but now all the messages were written by section B-1(a) of MI5.

The Abwehr put him in touch with two more German agents in England, whom we immediately nabbed. They also gave him a code and detailed wireless procedure, all of which was invaluable.

Snow was followed by Charlie, Rainbow, Summer, Biscuit, and eventually a small army of enemy spies, all in regular contact with Canaris, all apparently trusted by him, and all totally controlled by the British counterintelligence apparatus.

At that point MI5 began dimly to glimpse an awesome and tantalizing prospect: with a bit of luck, *they could control and manipulate the entire German espionage network in Britain.*

*   *   *

"Turning agents into double agents instead of hanging them
has two crucial advantages," Terry wound up. "Since the
enemy thinks his spies are still active, he doesn't try to
replace them with others who may not get caught. And,
since *we* are supplying the information the spies tell their
controllers, we can deceive the enemy and mislead his strat-
egists."

"It can't be that easy," said Godliman.

"Certainly not." Terry opened a window to let out the
fog of cigarette and pipe smoke. "To work, the system has
to be very near total. If there is any substantial number of
genuine agents here, their information will contradict that
of the double agents and the Abwehr will smell a rat."

"It sounds exciting," Godliman said. His pipe had gone
out.

Terry smiled for the first time that morning. "The people
here will tell you it's hard work—long hours, high tension,
frustration—but yes, of course it's exciting." He looked at
his watch. "Now I want you to meet a very bright young
member of my staff. Let me walk you to his office."

They went out of the room, up some stairs, and along
several corridors. "His name is Frederick Bloggs, and he
gets annoyed if you make jokes about it," Terry continued.
"We pinched him from Scotland Yard—he was an inspector with Special Branch. If you need arms and legs, use
him. You'll rank above him, of course, but I shouldn't
make too much of that—we don't, here. I suppose I hardly
need to say that to you."

They entered a small, bare room that looked out on to a
blank wall. There was no carpet. A photograph of a pretty
girl hung on the wall, and there was a pair of handcuffs on
the hat-stand.

Terry said, "Frederick Bloggs, Percival Godliman. I'll
leave you to it."

The man behind the desk was blond, stocky and short—
he must have been only just tall enough to get into the
police force, Godliman thought. His tie was an eyesore, but

he had a pleasant, open face and an attractive grin. His handshake was firm.

"Tell you what, Percy—I was just going to nip home for lunch," he said. "Why don't you come along? The wife makes a lovely sausage and chips." He had a broad cockney accent.

Sausage and chips was not Godliman's favorite meal, but he went along. They walked to Trafalgar Square and caught a bus to Hoxton. Bloggs said, "I married a wonderful girl, but she can't cook for nuts. I have sausage and chips every day."

East London was still smoking from the previous night's air raid. They passed groups of firemen and volunteers digging through rubble, playing hoses over dying fires and clearing debris from the streets. They saw an old man carry a precious radio out of a half-ruined house.

Godliman made conversation. "So we're to catch spies together."

"We'll have a go, Perce."

Bloggs's home was a three-bedroom semidetached house in a street of exactly similar houses. The tiny front gardens were all being used to grow vegetables. Mrs. Bloggs was the pretty girl in the photograph on the office wall. She looked tired. "She drives an ambulance during the raids, don't you, love?" Bloggs said. He was proud of her. Her name was Christine.

She said, "Every morning when I come home I wonder if the house will still be here."

"Notice it's the house she's worried about, not me," Bloggs said.

Godliman picked up a medal in a presentation case from the mantelpiece. "How did you get this?"

Christine answered. "He took a shotgun off a villain who was robbing a post office."

"You're quite a pair," Godliman said.

"You married, Percy?" Bloggs asked.

"I'm a widower."

"Sorry."

"My wife died of tuberculosis in 1930. We never had any children."

"We're not having any yet," Bloggs said. "Not while the world's in this state."

Christine said: "Oh, Fred, he's not interested in that!" She went out to the kitchen.

They sat around a square table in the center of the room to eat. Godliman was touched by this couple and the domestic scene, and found himself thinking of his Eleanor. That was unusual; he had been immune to sentiment for some years. Perhaps the nerves were coming alive again, at last. War did funny things.

Christine's cooking was truly awful. The sausages were burned. Bloggs drowned his meal in tomato ketchup and Godliman cheerfully followed suit.

When they got back to Whitehall Bloggs showed Godliman the file on unidentified enemy agents thought still to be operating in Britain.

There were three sources of information about such people. The first was the immigration records of the Home Office. Passport control had long been an arm of Military Intelligence, and there was a list—going back to the last war—of aliens who had entered the country but had not left or been accounted for in other ways, such as death or naturalization. At the outbreak of war they had all gone before tribunals that classified them in three groups. At first only "A" class aliens were interned; but by July of 1940, after some scaremongering by Fleet Service, the "B" and "C" classes were taken out of circulation. There was a small number of immigrants who could not be located, and it was a fair assumption that some of them were spies.

Their papers were in Bloggs's file.

The second source were wireless transmissions. Section C of MI8 patrolled the airwaves nightly, recorded everything they did not know for certain to be theirs, and passed it to the Government Code and Cipher School. This outfit, which had recently been moved from London's Berkeley Street to a country house at Bletchley Park, was not a school at all but a collection of chess champions, musicians, mathematicians and crossword puzzle enthusiasts dedicated to the belief that if a man could invent a code a man could crack it. Signals originating in the British Isles that could not be accounted for by any of the Services were assumed to be messages from spies.

The decoded messages were in Bloggs's file.

Finally there were the double agents, but their value was largely hoped-for rather than actual. Messages to them from the Abwehr had warned of several incoming agents, and had given away one resident spy—Mrs. Matilda Krafft of Bournemouth, who had sent money to Snow by post and was subsequently incarcerated in Holloway prison. But the doubles had not been able to reveal the identity or locations of the kind of quietly effective professional spies most valuable to a secret intelligence service. No one doubted that there were such people. There were clues—someone, for example, had brought Snow's transmitter over from Germany and deposited it in the cloakroom at Victoria Station for him to collect. But either the Abwehr or the spies themselves were too cautious to be caught by the doubles.

However the clues were in Bloggs's file.

Other sources were being developed: the experts were working to improve methods of triangulation (the directional pin-pointing of radio transmitters); and MI6 were trying to rebuild the networks of agents in Europe that had sunk beneath the tidal wave of Hitler's armies.

What little information there was was in Bloggs's file.

"It can be infuriating at times," he told Godliman. "Look at this."

He took from the file a long radio intercept about British plans for an expeditionary force for Finland. "This was picked up early in the year. The information is impeccable. They were trying to get a fix on him when he broke off in the middle, for no apparent reason—perhaps he was interrupted. He resumed a few minutes later, but he was off the air again before our people had a chance to plug in."

Godliman said, "What's this—'Regards to Willi'?"

"Now, that's important," said Bloggs. He was getting enthusiastic. "Here's a scrap of another message, quite recent. Look—'Regards to Willi.' This time there was a reply. He's addressed as 'Die Nadel.' "

"The Needle."

"This one's a pro. Look at his message: terse, economical, but detailed and completely unambiguous."

Godliman studied the fragment of the second message. "It appears to be about the effects of the bombing."

"He's obviously toured the East End. A pro, a pro."

"What else do we know about Die Nadel?"

Bloggs's expression of youthful eagerness collapsed. "That's it, I'm afraid."

"His code name is Die Nadel, he signs off 'Regards to Willi,' and he has good information—and that's it?"

" 'Fraid so."

Godliman sat on the edge of the desk and stared out of the window. On the wall of the opposite building, underneath an ornate window sill, he could see the nest of a house-marten. "On that basis, what chance have we of catching him?"

Bloggs shrugged. "On that basis, none at all."

5

IT IS FOR PLACES LIKE THIS THAT THE WORD "BLEAK" has been invented.

The island is a J-shaped lump of rock rising sullenly out of the North Sea. It lies on the map like the top half of a broken cane, parallel with the Equator but a long, long way north; its curved handle toward Aberdeen, its broken, jagged stump pointing threateningly at distant Denmark. It is ten miles long.

Around most of its coast the cliffs rise out of the cold sea without the courtesy of a beach. Angered by this rudeness the waves pound on the rock in impotent rage; a ten-thousand-year fit of bad temper that the island ignores with impunity.

In the cup of the J the sea is calmer; there it has provided itself with a more pleasant reception. Its tides have thrown into that cup so much sand and seaweed, driftwood and pebbles and seashells that there is now, between the foot of the cliff and the water's edge, a crescent of something closely resembling dry land, a more-or-less beach.

Each summer the vegetation at the top of the cliff drops a handful of seeds on to the beach, the way a rich man throws loose change to beggars. If the winter is mild and the spring comes early, a few of the seeds take feeble root; but they are never healthy enough to flower themselves and spread their own seeds, so the beach exists from year to year on handouts.

On the land itself, the proper land, held out of the sea's
reach by the cliffs, green things do grow and multiply. The
vegetation is mostly coarse grass, only just good enough to
nourish the few bony sheep, but tough enough to bind the
topsoil to the island's bedrock. There are some bushes, all
thorny, that provide homes for rabbits; and a brave stand
of conifers on the leeward slope of the hill at the eastern
end.

The higher land is ruled by heather. Every few years the
man—yes, there is a man here—sets fire to the heather,
and then the grass will grow and the sheep can graze here
too; but after a couple of years the heather comes back,
God knows from where, and drives the sheep away until
the man burns it again.

The rabbits are here because they were born here; the
sheep are here because they were brought here; and the man
is here to look after the sheep; but the birds are here because they like it. There are hundreds of thousands of them:
long-legged rock pipits whistling *peep peep peep* as they
soar and *pe-pe-pe-pe* as they dive like a Spitfire coming at
a Messerschmidt out of the sun; corncrakes, which the man
rarely sees, but he knows they are there because their bark
keeps him awake at night; ravens and carrion crows and
kittiwakes and *countless* gulls; and a pair of golden eagles
that the man shoots at when he sees them, for he *knows*—
regardless of what naturalists and experts from Edinburgh
may tell him—that they *do* prey on live lambs and not just
the carcasses of those already dead.

The island's most constant visitor is the wind. It comes
mostly from the northeast, from *really* cold places where
there are fjords and glaciers and icebergs; often bringing
with it unwelcome gifts of snow and driving rain and cold,
cold mist; sometimes arriving empty-handed, just to howl
and whoop and raise hell, tearing up bushes and bending
trees and whipping the intemperate ocean into fresh par-
oxysms of foam-flecked rage. It is tireless, this wind, and
that is its mistake. If it came occasionally it could take the

island by surprise and do some real damage; but because it is almost always here, the island has learned to live with it. The plants put down deep roots, and the rabbits hide far inside the thickets, and the trees grow up with their backs ready-bent for the flogging, and the birds nest on sheltered ledges, and the man's house is sturdy and squat, built with a craftsmanship that knows this old wind.

This house is made of big grey stones and grey slates, the color of the sea. It has small windows and close-fitting doors and a chimney in its pipe end. It stands at the top of the hill at the eastern end of the island, close to the splintered stub of the broken walking-stick. It crowns the hill, defying the wind and the rain, not out of bravado but so that the man can see the sheep.

There is another house, very similar, ten miles away at the opposite end of the island near the more-or-less beach; but nobody lives there. There was once another man. He thought he knew better than the island; he thought he could grow oats and potatoes and keep a few cows. He battled for three years with the wind and the cold and the soil before he admitted he was wrong. When he had gone, nobody wanted his home.

This is a hard place. Only hard things survive here: hard rock, coarse grass, tough sheep, savage birds, sturdy houses and strong men.

It is for places like this that the word "bleak" has been invented.

"It's called Storm Island," said Alfred Rose. "I think you're going to like it."

David and Lucy Rose sat in the prow of the fishing boat and looked across the choppy water. It was a fine November day, cold and breezy yet clear and dry. A weak sun sparkled off the wavelets.

"I bought it in 1926," Papa Rose continued, "when we thought there was going to be a revolution and we'd need somewhere to hide from the working class. It's just the place for a convalescence."

Lucy thought he was being suspiciously hearty, but she had to admit it looked lovely: all windblown and natural and fresh. And it made sense, this move. They had to get away from their parents and make a new start at being married; and there was no point in moving to a city to be bombed, not when neither of them was really well enough to help; and then David's father had revealed that he owned an island off the coast of Scotland, and it seemed too good to be true.

"I own the sheep, too," Papa Rose said. "Shearers come over from the mainland each spring, and the wool brings in just about enough money to pay Tom McAvity's wages. Old Tom's the shepherd."

"How old is he?" Lucy asked.

"Good Lord, he must be—oh, seventy?"

"I suppose he's eccentric." The boat turned into the bay, and Lucy could see two small figures on the jetty: a man and a dog.

"Eccentric? No more than you'd be if you'd lived alone for twenty years. He talks to his dog."

Lucy turned to the skipper of the small boat. "How often do you call?"

"Once a fortnight, missus. I bring Tom's shopping, which isna much, and his mail, which is even less. You just give me your list, every other Monday, and if it can be bought in Aberdeen I'll bring it."

He cut the motor and threw a rope to Tom. The dog barked and ran around in circles, beside himself with excitement. Lucy put one foot on the gunwale and sprang out on to the jetty.

Tom shook her hand. He had a face of leather and a huge pipe with a lid. He was shorter than she, but wide, and he looked ridiculously healthy. He wore the hairiest tweed jacket she had ever seen, with a knitted sweater that must have been made by an elderly sister somewhere, plus a checked cap and army boots. His nose was huge, red and veined. "Pleased to meet you," he said politely, as if she was his ninth visitor today instead of the first human face he had seen in fourteen days.

"Here y'are, Tom," said the skipper. He handed two cardboard boxes out of the boat. "No eggs this time, but there's a letter from Devon."

"It'll be from ma niece."

Lucy thought, That explains the sweater.

David was still in the boat. The skipper stood behind him and said, "Are you ready?"

Tom and Papa Rose leaned into the boat to assist, and the three of them lifted David in his wheelchair on to the jetty.

"If I don't go now I'll have to wait a fortnight for the next bus," Papa Rose said with a smile. "The house has been done up quite nicely, you'll see. All your stuff is in there. Tom will show you where everything is." He kissed Lucy, squeezed David's shoulder, and shook Tom's hand. "Have a few months of rest and togetherness, get completely fit, then come back; there are important war jobs for both of you."

They would not be going back, Lucy knew, not before the end of the war. But she had not told anyone about that yet.

Papa got back into the boat. It wheeled away in a tight circle. Lucy waved until it disappeared around the headland.

Tom pushed the wheelchair, so Lucy took his groceries. Between the landward end of the jetty and the cliff top was a long, steep, narrow ramp rising high above the beach like a bridge. Lucy would have had trouble getting the wheelchair to the top, but Tom managed without apparent exertion.

The cottage was perfect.

It was small and grey, and sheltered from the wind by a little rise in the ground. All the woodwork was freshly painted, and a wild rose bush grew beside the doorstep. Curls of smoke rose from the chimney to be whipped away by the breeze. The tiny windows looked over the bay.

Lucy said, "I love it!"

The interior had been cleaned and aired and painted, and there were thick rugs on the stone floors. It had four rooms: downstairs, a modernized kitchen and a living room with a stone fireplace; upstairs, two bedrooms. One end of the house had been carefully remodeled to take modern plumbing, with a bathroom above and a kitchen extension below.

Their clothes were in the wardrobes. There were towels in the bathroom and food in the kitchen.

Tom said, "There's something in the barn I've to show you."

It was a shed, not a barn. It lay hidden behind the cottage, and inside it was a gleaming new jeep.

"Mr. Rose says it's been specially adapted for young Mr. Rose to drive," Tom said. "It's got automatic gears, and the throttle and brake are operated by hand. That's what he said." He seemed to be repeating the words parrotfashion, as if he had very little idea of what gears, brakes and throttles might be.

Lucy said, "Isn't that super, David?"

"Top-hole. But where shall I go in it?"

Tom said: "You're always welcome to visit me and share a pipe and a drop of whisky. I've been looking forward to having neighbors again."

"Thank you," said Lucy.

"This here's the generator," Tom said, turning around and pointing. "I've got one just the same. You put the fuel in here. It delivers alternating current."

"That's unusual—small generators are usually direct current," David said.

"Aye. I don't really know the difference, but they tell me this is safer."

"True. A shock from this would throw you across the room, but direct current would kill you."

They went back to the cottage. Tom said, "Well, you'll want to settle in, and I've sheep to tend, so I'll say good-day. Oh! I ought to tell you—in an emergency, I can contact the mainland by wireless radio."

David was surprised. "You've got a radio transmitter?"

"Aye," Tom said proudly. "I'm an enemy aircraft spotter in the Royal Observer Corps."

"Ever spotted any?" David asked.

Lucy flashed her disapproval of the sarcasm in David's voice, but Tom seemed not to notice. "Not yet," he replied.

"Jolly good show."

When Tom had gone Lucy said, "He only wants to do his bit."

"There are lots of us who *want* to do our bit," David said.

And that, Lucy reflected, was the trouble. She dropped the subject, and wheeled her crippled husband into their new home.

When Lucy had been asked to visit the hospital psychologist, she had immediately assumed that David had brain damage. It was not so. "All that's wrong with his head is a nasty bruise on the left temple," the psychologist said. She went on: "However, the loss of both his legs is a trauma, and there's no telling how it will affect his state of mind. Did he want very much to be a pilot?"

Lucy pondered. "He was afraid, but I think he wanted it very badly, all the same."

"Well, he'll need all the reassurance and support that you can give him. And patience, too. One thing we can predict is that he will be resentful and ill-tempered for a while. He needs love and rest."

However, during their first few months on the island he seemed to want neither. He did not make love to her, perhaps because he was waiting until his injuries were fully healed. But he did not rest, either. He threw himself into the business of sheep farming, tearing about the island in his jeep with the wheelchair in the back. He built fences along the more treacherous cliffs, shot at the eagles, helped Tom train a new dog when Betsy began to go blind, and burned off the heather; and in the spring he was out every night delivering lambs. One day he felled a great old pine tree near Tom's cottage, and spent a fortnight stripping it, hewing it into manageable logs and carting them back to the house for firewood. He relished really hard manual labor. He learned to strap himself tightly to the chair to keep his body anchored while he wielded an axe or a mallet. He carved a pair of Indian clubs and exercised with them for hours when Tom could find nothing more for him to do. The muscles of his arms and back became near-grotesque, like those of men who win body-building contests.

Lucy was not unhappy. She had been afraid he might sit by the fire all day and brood over his bad luck. The way he worked was faintly worrying because it was so obsessive, but at least he was not vegetating.

She told him about the baby at Christmas.

In the morning she gave him a gasoline-driven saw, and he gave her a bolt of silk. Tom came over for dinner, and they ate a wild goose he had shot. David drove the shepherd home after tea, and when he came back Lucy opened a bottle of brandy.

Then she said, "I have another present for you, but you can't open it until May."

He laughed. "What on earth are you talking about? How much of that brandy did you drink while I was out?"

"I'm having a baby."

He stared at her, and all the laughter went out of his face. "Good God, that's all we bloody well need."

"David!"

"Well, for God's sake. . . . When the hell did it happen?"

"That's not too difficult to figure out, is it?" she said. "It must have been a week before the wedding. It's a miracle it survived the crash."

"Have you seen a doctor?"

"Huh—when?"

"So how do you know for sure?"

"Oh, David, don't be so boring. I know for sure because my periods have stopped and my nipples hurt and I throw up in the mornings and my waist is four inches bigger than it used to be. If you ever *looked* at me *you* would know for sure."

"All right."

"What's the matter with you? You're supposed to be thrilled!"

"Oh, sure. Perhaps we'll have a son, and then I can take him for walks and play football with him, and he'll grow up wanting to be like his father the war hero, a legless fucking joke!"

"Oh, David, David," she whispered. She knelt in front of his wheelchair. "David, don't think like that. He will respect you. He'll look up to you because you put your life together again, and because you can do the work of two men from your wheelchair, and because you carried your disability with courage and cheerfulness and—"

"Don't be so damned condescending," he snapped. "You sound like a sanctimonious priest."

She stood up. "Well, don't act as if it's my fault. Men can take precautions too, you know."

"Not against invisible trucks in the blackout!"

It was a silly exchange and they both knew it, so Lucy said nothing. The whole idea of Christmas seemed utterly trite now: the bits of colored paper on the walls, and the tree in the corner, and the remains of a goose in the kitchen waiting to be thrown away—none of it had anything to do with her life. She began to wonder what she was doing on this bleak island with a man who seemed not to love her, having a baby he didn't want. Why shouldn't she—why not—well, she could. . . . Then she realized she had no-where else to go, nothing else to do with her life, nobody else to *be* other than Mrs. David Rose.

Eventually David said, "Well, I'm going to bed." He

wheeled himself to the hall and dragged himself out of the chair and up the stairs backwards. She heard him scrape across the floor, heard the bed creak as he hauled himself on to it, heard his clothes hit the corner of the room as he undressed, then heard the final groaning of the springs as he lay down and pulled the blankets up over him.

And still she would not cry.

She looked at the brandy bottle and thought, If I drink all of this now, and have a bath, perhaps I won't be pregnant in the morning.

She thought about it for a long time, until she came to the conclusion that life without David and the island and the baby would be even worse because it would be empty.

So she did not cry, and she did not drink the brandy, and she did not leave the island; but instead she went upstairs and got into bed, and lay awake beside her sleeping husband, listening to the wind and trying not to think, until the gulls began to call, and a grey rainy dawn crept over the North Sea and filled the little bedroom with a cold pale light, and at last she went to sleep.

A kind of peace settled over her in the spring, as if all threats were postponed until after the baby was born. When the February snow had thawed she planted flowers and vegetables in the patch of ground between the kitchen door and the barn, not really believing they would grow. She cleaned the house thoroughly and told David that if he wanted it done again before August he would have to do it himself. She wrote to her mother and did a lot of knitting and ordered diapers by mail. They suggested she go home to have the baby, but she knew, was afraid, that if she went she would never come back. She went for long walks over the moors, with a bird book under her arm, until her weight became too much for her to carry very far. She kept the bottle of brandy in a cupboard David never used, and whenever she felt depressed she went to look at it and remind herself of what she had almost lost.

Three weeks before the baby was due, she got the boat

into Aberdeen. David and Tom waved from the jetty. The sea was so rough that both she and the skipper were terrified she might give birth before they reached the mainland. She went into the hospital in Aberdeen, and four weeks later brought the baby home on the same boat.

David knew none of it. He probably thought that women gave birth as easily as ewes, she decided. He was oblivious to the pain of contractions, and that awful, impossible stretching, and the soreness afterward, and the bossy, know-it-all nurses who didn't want you to touch your baby because you weren't brisk and efficient and trained and sterile like they were; he just saw you go away pregnant and come back with a beautiful, white-wrapped, healthy baby boy and said, "We'll call him Jonathan."

They added Alfred for David's father, and Malcolm for Lucy's, and Thomas for old Tom, but they called the boy Jo, because he was too tiny for Jonathan, let alone Jonathan Alfred Malcolm Thomas Rose. David learned to give him his bottle and burp him and change his diaper, and he even dangled him in his lap occasionally, but his interest seemed distant, uninvolved; he had a problem-solving approach, like the nurses; it was not for him as it was for Lucy. Tom was closer to the baby than David. Lucy would not let him smoke in the room where the baby was, and the old boy would put his great briar pipe with the lid in his pocket for hours and gurgle at little Jo, or watch him kick his feet, or help Lucy bathe him. Lucy suggested mildly that he might be neglecting the sheep. Tom said they did not need him to watch them feed—he would rather watch Jo feed. He carved a rattle out of driftwood and filled it with small round pebbles, and was overjoyed when Jo grabbed it and shook it, first time, without having to be shown how.

David and Lucy still did not make love.

First there had been his injuries, and then she had been pregnant, and then she had been recovering from childbirth; but now the reasons had run out.

One night she said, "I'm back to normal now."

"How do you mean?"

"After the baby. My body is normal. I've healed."

"Oh, I see. That's good."

She made sure to go to bed with him so that he could watch her undress, but he always turned his back.

As they lay there, dozing off, she would move so that her hand, or her thigh, or her breast, brushed against him, a casual but unmistakable invitation. There was no response.

She believed firmly that there was nothing wrong with her. She wasn't a nymphomaniac—she didn't simply want sex, she wanted sex with David. She was sure that, even if there had been another man under seventy on the island, she would not have been tempted. She wasn't a sex-starved tart, she was a love-starved wife.

The crunch came on one of those nights when they lay on their backs, side by side, both wide awake, listening to the wind outside and the small sounds of Jo from the next room. It seemed to Lucy that it was time he either did it or came right out and said why not; and that he was going to avoid the issue until she forced it; and that she might as well force it now.

So she brushed her arm across his thighs and opened her mouth to speak—and almost cried out with shock to discover that he had an erection. So he he could do it! And he wanted to, or why else—and her hand closed triumphantly around the evidence of his desire, and she shifted closer to him, and sighed, "David—"

He said, "Oh, for God's sake!" and gripped her wrist and pushed her hand away from him and turned onto his side.

But this time she was not going to accept his rebuff in modest silence. "David, why not?"

"Jesus Christ!" He threw the blankets off, swung himself to the floor, grabbed the eiderdown with one hand, and dragged himself to the door.

Lucy sat up in bed and screamed at him, "Why not?"

Jo began to cry.

David pulled up the empty legs of his cut-off pajama trousers, pointed to the pursed white skin of his stumps, and said, "That's why not! That's why not!"

He slithered downstairs to sleep on the sofa, and Lucy went into the next bedroom to comfort Jo.

It took a long time to lull him back to sleep, probably because she herself was so much in need of comfort. The baby tasted the tears on her cheeks, and she wondered if he had any inkling of their meaning—wouldn't tears be one of the first things a baby came to understand? She could not bring herself to sing to him, or murmur that everything was all right; so she held him tight and rocked him, and when *he* had soothed *her* with his warmth and his clinging, he went to sleep in her arms.

She put him back in the cot and stood looking at him for a while. There was no point in going back to bed. She could hear David's deep-sleep snoring from the living room—he had to take powerful pills, otherwise the old pain kept him awake. Lucy needed to get away from him, where she could neither see nor hear him, where he couldn't find her for a few hours even if he wanted to. She put on trousers and a sweater, a heavy coat and boots, and crept downstairs and out.

There was a swirling mist, damp and bitterly cold, the kind the island specialized in. She put up the collar of her coat, thought about going back inside for a scarf, and decided not to. She squelched along the muddy path, welcoming the bite of the fog in her throat, the small discomfort of the weather taking her mind off the larger hurt inside her.

She reached the cliff top and walked gingerly down the steep, narrow ramp, placing her feet carefully on the slippery boards. At the bottom she jumped off on the sand and walked to the edge of the sea.

The wind and the water were carrying on their perpetual quarrel, the wind swooping down to tease the waves and the sea hissing and spitting as it crashed against the land, the two of them doomed to bicker forever.

Lucy walked along the hard sand, letting the noise and the weather fill her head, until the beach ended in a sharp point where the water met the cliff, when she turned and walked back. She paced the shore all night. Toward dawn a thought came to her, unbidden: It is his way of being strong.

As it was, the thought was not much help, holding its meaning in a tightly clenched fist. But she worked on it for a while, and the fist opened to reveal what looked like a small pearl of wisdom nestling in its palm—perhaps David's coldness to her was of one piece with his chopping down trees, and undressing himself, and driving the jeep, and throwing the Indian clubs, and coming to live on a cold cruel island in the North Sea . . .

What was it he had said? ". . . his father the war hero, a legless joke . . ." He had something to prove, something that would sound trite if it were put into words; something he could have done as a fighter pilot, but now had to do with trees and fences and Indian clubs and a wheelchair. They wouldn't let him take the test, and he wanted to be able to say: "I could have passed it anyway, just *look* how I can suffer."

It was cruelly, screamingly unjust: he had had the courage, and he had suffered the wounds, but he could take no pride in it. If a Messerschmidt had taken his legs the wheelchair would have been like a medal, a badge of courage. But now, all his life, he would have to say: "It was during the war—but no, I never saw any action, this was a car crash. I did my training and I was going to fight, the very next day, I had seen my kite, she was a beauty, and . . ."

Yes, it was his way of being strong. And perhaps she could be strong, too. She might find ways of patching up the wreck of her life. David had once been good and kind and loving, and she might now learn to wait patiently while he battled to become the complete man he used to be. She could find new hopes, new things to live for. Other women had found the strength to cope with bereavement, and bombed-out houses, and husbands in prisoner-of-war camps.

She picked up a pebble, drew back her arm, and threw it out to sea with all her might. She did not see or hear it land; it might have gone on forever, circling the earth like a satellite in a space story.

She shouted, "I can be strong, too, damn it." And then she turned around and started up the ramp to the cottage. It was almost time for Jo's first feed.

6

IT LOOKED LIKE A MANSION, AND, UP TO A POINT, that was what it was—a large house, in its own grounds, in the leafy town of Wohldorf just outside North Hamburg. It might have been the home of a mine owner, or a successful importer, or an industrialist. However, it was in fact owned by the Abwehr.

It owed its fate to the weather—not here, but two hundred miles southeast in Berlin, where atmospheric conditions were unsuitable for wireless communication with England.

It was a mansion only down to ground level. Below that were two huge concrete shelters and several million reichsmarks' worth of radio equipment. The electronics system had been put together by a Major Werner Trautmann, and he did a good job. Each hall had twenty neat little soundproof listening posts, occupied by radio operators who could recognize a spy by the way he tapped out his message, as easily as you can recognize your mother's handwriting on an envelope.

The receiving equipment was built with quality in mind, for the transmitters sending the messages had been designed for compactness rather than power. Most of them were the small suitcase-sets called Klamotten, which had been developed by Telefunken for Admiral Wilhelm Canaris, the head of the Abwehr.

On this night the airways were relatively quiet, so every

one knew when Die Nadel came through. The message was taken by one of the older operators. He tapped out an acknowledgment, transcribed the signal, quickly tore the sheet off his note pad and went to the phone. He read the message over the direct line to Abwehr headquarters at Sophien Terrace in Hamburg, then came back to his booth for a smoke.

He offered a cigarette to the youngster in the next booth, and the two of them stood together for a few minutes, leaning against the wall and smoking.

The youngster said, "Anything?"

The older man shrugged. "There's always *something* when he calls. But not much this time. The Luftwaffe missed St. Paul's Cathedral again."

"No reply for him?"

"We don't think he waits for replies. He's an independent bastard, always was. I trained him in wireless, you know, and once I'd finished he thought he knew it better than me."

"You've *met* Die Nadel? What's he like?"

"About as much fun as a dead fish. All the same he's the best agent we've got. Some say the best ever. There's a story that he spent five years working his way up in the NKVD in Russia, and ended up one of Stalin's most trusted aides. . . . I don't know whether it's true, but it's the kind of thing he'd do. A real pro. And the Fuehrer knows it."

"Hitler knows him?"

The older man nodded. "At one time he wanted to see all Die Nadel's signals. I don't know if he still does. Not that it would make any difference to Die Nadel. Nothing impresses that man. You know something? He looks at everybody the same way—as if he's figuring out how he'll kill you if you make a wrong move."

"I'm glad I didn't have to train him."

"He learned quickly, I'll give him that. Worked at it twenty-four hours a day, then when he'd mastered it, he wouldn't give me a good-morning. It takes him all his time to remember to salute Canaris. He always signs off 'Regards to Willi.' That's how much he cares about rank."

They finished their cigarettes, dropped them on the floor, and trod them out. Then the older man picked up the stubs and pocketed them, because smoking was not really permitted in the dugout. The radios were still quiet.

"Yes, he won't use his code name," the older man went on. "Von Braun gave it to him, and he's never liked it. He's never liked Von Braun either. Do you remember the time—no, it was before you joined us—Braun told Nadel to go to the airfield in Farnborough, Kent. The message came back: 'There is no airfield in Farnborough, Kent. There is one at Farnborough, Hampshire. Fortunately the Luftwaffe's geography is better than yours, you cunt.' Just like that."

"I suppose it's understandable. When we make mistakes we put their lives on the line."

The older man frowned. He was the one who delivered such judgments, and he did not like his audience to weigh in with opinions of its own. "Perhaps," he said grudgingly.

"But why doesn't he like his code name?"

"He says it has a meaning, and a code word with a meaning can give a man away. Von Braun wouldn't listen."

"A meaning? The Needle? What does it mean?"

But at that moment the old-timer's radio chirped, and he returned quickly to his station, so the explanation never came.

PART TWO

7

THE MESSAGE ANNOYED FABER BECAUSE IT FORCED
him to face issues that he had been avoiding.

Hamburg had made damn sure the message reached
him. He had given his call-sign, and instead of the usual
"Acknowledge—proceed" they had sent back "Make rendezvous one."

He acknowledged the order, transmitted his report and
packed the wireless set back into its suitcase. Then he
wheeled his bicycle out of Erith Marshes—his cover was
a bird-watcher—and got on the road to Blackheath. As he
cycled back to his cramped two-room flat, he wondered
whether to obey the order.

He had two reasons for disobedience: one professional,
one personal.

The professional reason was that "rendezvous one" was
an old code, set up by Canaris back in 1937. It meant he
was to go to the doorway of a certain shop between Leicester Square and Piccadilly Circus to meet another agent. The
agents would recognize each other by the fact that they both
carried a Bible. Then there was a patter:

"What is today's chapter?"

"One Kings thirteen."

Then, if they were certain they were not being followed,
they would agree that the chapter was "most inspiring."
Otherwise one would say, "I'm afraid I haven't read it yet."

The shop doorway might not be there any more, but it

was not that that troubled Faber. He thought Canaris had probably given the code to most of the bumbling amateurs who had crossed the Channel in 1940 and landed in the arms of MI5. Faber knew they had been caught because the hangings had been publicized, no doubt to reassure the public that something was being done about Fifth Columnists. They would certainly have given away secrets before they died, so the British now probably knew the old rendezvous code. If they had picked up the message from Hamburg, that shop doorway must by now be swarming with well-spoken young Englishmen carrying Bibles and practicing saying "Most inspiring" in a German accent.

The Abwehr had thrown professionalism to the wind back in those heady days when the invasion seemed so close. Faber had not trusted Hamburg since. He would not tell them where he lived, he refused to communicate with their other agents in Britain, he varied the frequency he used for transmission without caring whether he stepped all over someone else's signal.

If he had always obeyed his masters, he would not have survived so long.

At Woolwich, Faber was joined by a mass of other cyclists, many of them women, as the workers came streaming out of the munitions factory at the end of the day shift. Their cheerful weariness reminded Faber of his personal reason for disobedience: he thought his side was losing the war.

They certainly were not winning. The Russians and the Americans had joined in, Africa was lost, the Italians had collapsed; the Allies would surely invade France this year, 1944.

Faber did not want to risk his life to no purpose.

He arrived home and put his bicycle away. While he was washing his face it dawned on him that, against all logic, he *wanted* to make the rendezvous.

It was a foolish risk, taken in a lost cause, but he was itching to get to it. And the simple reason was that he was unspeakably bored. The routine transmissions, the bird-watching, the bicycle, the boardinghouse teas—it was four years since he had experienced anything remotely like action. He seemed to be in no danger whatsoever, and that made him jumpy because he imagined invisible threats. He was happiest when every so often he could identify a threat and take steps to neutralize it.

Yes, he would make the rendezvous. But not in the way they expected.

There were still crowds in the West End of London, despite the war; Faber wondered whether it was the same in Berlin. He bought a Bible at Hatchard's bookshop in Piccadilly, and stuffed it into his inside coat pocket, out of sight. It was a mild, damp day, with intermittent drizzle, and Faber was carrying an umbrella.

This rendezvous was timed for either between nine and ten o'clock in the morning or between five and six in the afternoon, and the arrangement was that one went there every day until the other party turned up. If no contact was made for five successive days one went there on alternate days for two weeks. After that one gave up.

Faber got to Leicester Square at ten past nine. The contact was there, in the tobacconist's doorway, with a black-bound Bible under his arm, pretending to shelter from the rain. Faber spotted him out of the corner of his eye and hurried past, head down. The man was youngish, with a blond moustache and a well-fed look. He wore a black double-breasted raincoat, and he was reading the *Daily Express* and chewing gum. He was not familiar.

When Faber walked by the second time on the opposite side of the street, he spotted the tail. A short, stocky man wearing the trenchcoat and trilby hat beloved of English plainclothes policemen was standing just inside the foyer of an office building, looking through the glass doors across the street to the man in the doorway.

There were two possibilities. If the agent did not know

he had been followed, Faber had only to get him away from
the rendezvous and lose the tail. However, the alternative
was that the agent had been captured and the man in the
doorway was a substitute, in which case neither he nor the
tail must be allowed to see Faber's face.

Faber assumed the worst, then thought of a way to deal
with it.

There was a telephone booth in the Square. Faber went
inside and memorized the number. Then he found I Kings
13 in the Bible, tore out the page, and scribbled in the
margin, "Go to the phone booth in the Square."

He walked around the back streets behind the National
Gallery until he found a small boy, aged about ten or
eleven, sitting on a doorstep throwing stones at puddles.

Faber said, "Do you know the tobacconist in the
Square?"

"Yerst."

"Do you like chewing gum?"

"Yerst."

Faber gave him a page torn from the Bible. "There's a
man in the doorway of the tobacconist's. If you give him
this he'll give you some gum."

"All right," the boy said. He stood up. "Is this geezer a
Yank?"

"Yerst," Faber said.

The boy ran off. Faber followed him. As the boy approached the agent, Faber ducked into the doorway of the
building opposite. The tail was still there, peering through
the glass. Faber stood just outside the door, blocking the
tail's view of the scene across the street, and opened his
umbrella. He pretended to be struggling with it. He saw the
agent give something to the boy and walked off. He ended
his charade with the umbrella and walked in the direction
opposite to the way the agent had gone. He looked back
over his shoulder to see the tail run into the street, looking
for the vanished agent.

Faber stopped at the nearest telephone and dialed the

number of the booth in the Square. It took a few minutes
to get through. At last a deep voice said, "Hello?"

"What is today's chapter?" Faber said.

"One Kings thirteen."

"Most inspiring."

"Yes, isn't it."

The fool has no idea of the trouble he's in, Faber thought.
Aloud he said, "Well?"

"I must see you."

"That is impossible."

"But I must!" There was a note in the voice that Faber
thought edged on despair. "The message comes from the
very top—do you understand?"

Faber pretended to waver. "All right, then. I will meet
you in one week's time under the arch at Euston Station at
9 A.M."

"Can't you make it sooner?"

Faber hung up and stepped outside. Walking quickly, he
rounded two corners and came within sight of the phone
booth in the Square. He saw the agent walking in the direction of Piccadilly. There was no sign of the tail. Faber
followed the agent.

The man went into Piccadilly Circus underground station, and bought a ticket to Stockwell. Faber immediately
realized he could get there by a more direct route. He came
out of the station, walked quickly to Leicester Square and
got on a Northern Line train. The agent would have to
change trains at Waterloo, whereas Faber's train was direct;
so Faber would reach Stockwell first, or at the worst they
would arrive on the same train.

In fact Faber had to wait outside the station at Stockwell
for twenty-five minutes before the agent emerged. Faber
followed him again. He went into a cafe.

There was absolutely nowhere nearby where a man could
plausibly stand still for any length of time: no shop windows to gaze into, no benches to sit on or parks to walk
around, no bus stops or taxi ranks or public buildings. Faber

had to walk up and down the street, always looking as if he were going somewhere, carrying on until he was just out of sight of the cafe then returning on the opposite side, while the agent sat in the warm, steamy cafe drinking tea and eating hot toast.

He came out after half an hour. Faber tailed him through a succession of residential streets. The agent knew where he was going, but was in no hurry. He walked like a man who is going home with nothing to do for the rest of the day. He did not look back, and Faber thought, Another amateur.

At last he went into a house—one of the poor, anonymous, inconspicuous lodging houses used by spies and errant husbands everywhere. It had a dormer window in the roof; that would be the agent's room, high up for better wireless reception.

Faber walked past, scanning the opposite side of the street. Yes—there. A movement behind an upstairs window, a glimpse of a jacket and tie, a watching face withdrawn—the opposition was here too. The agent must have gone to the rendezvous yesterday and allowed himself to be followed home by MI5—unless, of course, he *was* MI5.

Faber turned the corner and walked down the next parallel street, counting the houses. Almost directly behind the place the agent had entered there was the bomb-damaged shell of what had been a pair of semidetached houses. Good.

As he walked back to the station his step was springier, his heart beat a shade faster and he looked around him with bright-eyed interest. It was good. The game was on.

He dressed in black that night—a woolen hat, a turtleneck sweater under a short leather flying jacket, trousers tucked into socks, rubber-soled shoes—all black. He would be almost invisible, for London, too, was blacked out.

He cycled through the quiet streets with dimmed lights, keeping off main roads. It was after midnight, and he saw no one. He left the bike a quarter of a mile away from his destination, padlocking it to the fence in a pub yard.

He went, not to the agent's house, but to the bombed-out shell in the next street. He picked his way carefully across the rubble in the front garden, entered the gaping doorway, and went through the house to the back. It was very dark. A thick screen of low cloud hid the moon and stars. Faber had to walk slowly with his hands in front of him.

He reached the end of the garden, jumped over the fence, and crossed the next two gardens. In one of the houses a dog barked for a moment.

The garden of the lodging house was unkempt. Faber walked into a blackberry bush and stumbled. The thorns scratched his face. He ducked under a line of washing—there was enough light for him to see that.

He found the kitchen window and took from his pocket a small tool with a scoop-shaped blade. The putty around the glass was old and brittle, and already flaking away in places. After twenty minutes' silent work he took the pane out of the frame and laid it gently on the grass. He shone a flashlight through the empty hole to make sure there were no noisy obstacles in his way, opened the catch, raised the window and then climbed in.

The darkened house smelled of boiled fish and disinfectant. Faber unlocked the back door—a precaution for fast exit—before entering the hall. He flashed his pencil light on and off quickly, once. In that instant of light he took in a tiled hallway, a kidney table he must circumvent, a row of coats on hooks and a staircase, to the right, carpeted.

He climbed the stairs silently.

He was halfway across the landing to the second flight when he saw the light under the door. A split-second later there was an asthmatic cough and the sound of a toilet flushing. Faber reached the door in two strides and froze against the wall.

Light flooded the landing as the door opened. Faber

slipped his stiletto out of his sleeve. The old man came out of the toilet and crossed the landing, leaving the light on. At his bedroom door he grunted, turned and came back.

He must see me, Faber thought. He tightened his grip on the handle of his knife. The old man's half-open eyes were directed on the floor. He looked up as he reached for the light cord, and Faber almost killed him then—but the man fumbled for the switch and Faber realized he was so sleepy he was practically somnambulating.

The light died, the old man shuffled back to bed, and Faber breathed again.

There was only one door at the top of the second flight of stairs. Faber tried it gently. It was locked.

He took another tool from the pocket of his jacket. The noise of the toilet tank filling covered the sound of Faber picking the lock. He opened the door and listened.

He could hear deep regular breathing. He stepped inside. The sound came from the opposite corner of the room. He could see nothing. He crossed the pitch-dark room very slowly, feeling the air in front of him at each step, until he was beside the bed.

He had the flashlight in his left hand, the stiletto loose in his sleeve and his right hand free. He switched on the flashlight and grabbed the sleeping man's throat in a strangling grip.

The agent's eyes snapped open, but he could make no sound. Faber straddled the bed and sat on him. Then he whispered, "One Kings thirteen," and relaxed his grip.

The agent peered into the flashlight, trying to see Faber's face. He rubbed his neck where Faber's hand had squeezed.

"Be still!" Faber shone the light into the agent's eyes, and with his right hand drew the stiletto.

"Aren't you going to let me get up?"

"I prefer you in bed where you can do no more damage."

"Damage? More damage?"

"You were watched in Leicester Square, and you let me

follow you here, and they are observing this house. Should I trust you to do anything?"

"My God, I'm sorry."

"Why did they send you?"

"The message had to be delivered personally. The orders come from the top. The very top—" The agent stopped.

"Well? What orders?"

"I . . . have to be sure it's you."

"How can you be sure?"

"I must see your face."

Faber hesitated, then shone the flashlight at himself briefly. "Satisfied?"

"Die Nadel."

"And who are you?"

"Major Friedrich Kaldor, sir."

"I should call you Sir."

"Oh, no, sir. You've been promoted twice in your absence. You are now a lieutenant-colonel."

"Have they really nothing better to do in Hamburg?"

"Aren't you pleased?"

"I should be pleased to go back and put Major von Braun on latrine duty."

"May I get up, sir?"

"Certainly not. What if Major Kaldor is held in Wandsworth Jail and you are a substitute, waiting to give a signal to your watching friends in the house opposite? . . . Now, what are these orders from the very top?"

"Well, sir, we believe there will be an invasion of France this year."

"Brilliant, brilliant. Go on."

"They believe that General Patton is massing the First United States Army Group in the part of England known as East Anglia. If that army is the invasion force, then it follows that they will attack via the Pas de Calais."

"That makes sense. But I have seen no sign of this army of Patton's."

"There is some doubt in the highest circles in Berlin. The Fuehrer's astrologer—"

"What?"

"Yes, sir, he has an astrologer, who tells him to defend Normandy."

"My God. Are things that bad there?"

"He gets plenty of earthbound advice, too. I personally believe he uses the astrologer as an excuse when he thinks the generals are wrong but he can't fault their arguments."

Faber sighed. He had been afraid of news like this. "Go on."

"Your assignment is to assess the strength of FUSAG: numbers of troops, artillery, air support—"

"I know how to measure armies."

"Of course." He paused. "I am instructed to emphasize the importance of the mission, sir."

"And you have done so. Tell me, are things that bad in Berlin?"

The agent hesitated. "No, sir. Morale is high, output of munitions increases every month, the people spit at the RAF bombers—"

"Never mind, I can get the propaganda from my radio."

The younger man was silent.

Faber said, "Do you have anything else to tell me? Officially, I mean."

"Yes. For the duration of the assignment you have a special bolt-hole."

"They *do* think it's important," Faber said.

"You rendezvous with a U-boat in the North Sea, ten miles due east of a town called Aberdeen. Just call them in on your normal radio frequency and they will surface. As soon as you or I have told Hamburg that the orders have been passed from me to you, the route will be open. The boat will be there every Friday and Monday at 6 P.M. and will wait until 6 A.M."

"Aberdeen is a big town. Do you have an exact map reference?"

"Yes." The agent recited the numbers, and Faber memorized them.

"Is that everything, Major?"

"Yes, sir."

"What do you plan to do about the gentlemen from MI5 in the house across the road?"

The agent shrugged. "I'll have to give them the slip."

Faber thought, It's no good. "What are your orders after you have seen me? Do you have a bolt-hole?"

"No. I am to go to a town called Weymouth and steal a boat to return to France."

That was no plan at all. So, Faber thought, Canaris knew how it would be. Very well.

"And if you are caught by the British and tortured?" he said.

"I have a suicide pill."

"And you will use it?"

"Most certainly."

Faber looked at him. "I think you might," he said. He placed his left hand on the agent's chest and put his weight on it, as if he were about to get off the bed. That way he was able to feel exactly where the rib cage ended and the soft belly began. He thrust the point of the stiletto in just under the ribs and stabbed upward to the heart.

The agent's eyes widened for an instant. A noise came to his throat but did not get out. His body convulsed. Faber pushed the stiletto an inch farther in. The eyes closed and the body went limp.

"You saw my face," Faber said.

8

"I THINK WE'VE LOST CONTROL OF IT," SAID PERCI-
val Godliman. Frederick Bloggs nodded agreement, and
added, "It's my fault."

The man looked weary, Godliman thought. He had had
that look for almost a year, ever since the night they had
dragged the crushed remains of his wife from underneath
the rubble of a bombed house in Hoxton.

"I'm not interested in apportioning blame," Godliman
said. "The fact is that something happened in Leicester
Square during the few seconds you lost sight of Blondie."

"Do you think the contact was made?"

"Possibly."

"When we picked him up again in Stockwell, I thought
he had simply given up for the day."

"If that were the case he would have made the rendezvous again yesterday and today." Godliman was making
patterns with matchsticks on his desk, a thinking habit he
had developed. "Still no movement at the house?"

"Nothing. He's been in there for forty-eight hours."
Bloggs repeated, "It's my fault."

"Don't be a bore, old chap," Godliman said. "It was my
decision to let him run so that he would lead us to someone
else, and I still think it was the right move."

Bloggs sat motionless, his expression blank, his hands in
the pockets of his raincoat. "If the contact has been made,
we shouldn't delay picking Blondie up and finding out what
his mission was."

"That way we lose whatever chance we have of following Blondie to somebody more important."

"Your decision."

Godliman had made a church with his matches. He stared at it for a moment, then took a halfpenny from his pocket and tossed it. "Tails," he observed. "Give him another twenty-four hours."

The landlord was a middle-aged Irish Republican from Lisdoonvarna, County Clare, who harbored a secret hope that the Germans would win the war and thus free the Emerald Isle from English oppression forever. He limped arthritically around the old house, collecting his weekly rents, thinking how much he would be worth if those rents were allowed to rise to their true market value. He was not a rich man—he owned only two houses, this and the smaller one in which he lived. He was permanently bad-tempered.

On the first floor he tapped on the door of the old man. This tenant was always pleased to see him. He was probably pleased to see anybody. He said, "Hello, Mr. Riley, would you like a cup of tea?"

"No time today."

"Oh, well." The old man handed over the money. "I expect you've seen the kitchen window."

"No, I didn't go in there."

"Oh! Well, there's a pane of glass out. I patched it over with blackout curtain, but of course there is a draft."

"Who smashed it?" the landlord asked.

"Funny thing, it ain't broke. Just lying there on the grass. I expect the old putty just gave way. I'll mend it myself, if you can get hold of a bit of putty."

You old fool, the landlord thought. Aloud he said, "I don't suppose it occurred to you that you might have been burgled?"

The old man looked astonished. "I never thought of that."

"Nobody's missing any valuables?"

"Nobody's said so to me."

The landlord went to the door. "All right, I'll have a look when I go down."

The old man followed him out. "I don't think the new bloke is in upstairs," he said. "I haven't heard a sound for a couple of days."

The landlord was sniffing. "Has he been cooking in his room?"

"I wouldn't know, Mr. Riley."

The two of them went up the stairs. The old man said, "He's very quiet, if he is in there."

"Whatever he's cooking, he'll have to stop. It smells bloody awful."

The landlord knocked on the door. There was no answer. He opened it and went in, and the old man followed him.

"Well, well, well," the old sergeant said heartily. "I think you've got a dead one." He stood in the doorway, surveying the room. "You touched anything, Paddy?"

"No," the landlord replied. "And the name's Mr. Riley."

The policeman ignored this. "Not long dead, though. I've smelled worse." His survey took in the old chest of drawers, the suitcase on the low table, the faded square of carpet, the dirty curtains on the dormer window and the rumpled bed in the corner. There were no signs of a struggle.

He went over to the bed. The young man's face was peaceful, his hands clasped over his chest. "I'd say heart attack, if he wasn't so young." There was no empty sleeping-pill bottle to indicate suicide. He picked up the leather wallet on top of the chest and looked through its contents. There was an identity card and a ration book, and a fairly thick wad of notes. "Papers in order and he ain't been robbed."

"He's only been here a week or so," the landlord said. "I don't know much about him at all. He came from North Wales to work in a factory."

"Well," the sergeant observed, "if he was as healthy as

he looked he'd be in the Army." He opened the suitcase on the table. "Bloody hell, what's this lot?"

The landlord and the old man had edged their way into the room now. The landlord said, "It's a radio" at the same time as the old man said, "He's bleeding."

"Don't touch that body!" the sergeant said.

"He's had a knife in the guts," the old man persisted.

The sergeant gingerly lifted one of the dead hands from the chest to reveal a small trickle of dried blood. "He *was* bleeding," he said. "Where's the nearest phone?"

"Five doors down," the landlord told him.

"Lock this room and stay out until I get back."

The sergeant left the house and knocked at the door of the neighbor with the phone. A woman opened it. "Good morning, madam. May I use your telephone?"

"Come in." She showed him the phone, on a stand in the hall. "What's happened—anything exciting?"

"A tenant died in a lodging house just up the road," he told her as he dialed.

"Murdered?" she asked, wide-eyed.

"I leave that to the experts. Hello? Superintendent Jones, please. This is Canter." He looked at the woman. "Might I ask you just to pop in the kitchen while I talk to my governor?"

She went, disappointed.

"Hello, Super. This body's got a knife wound and a suitcase radio."

"What's the address again, Sarge?"

Sergeant Canter told him.

"Yes, that's the one they've been watching. This is an MI5 job, Sarge. Go to number 42 and tell the surveillance team there what you've found. I'll get on to their chief. Off you go."

Canter thanked the woman and crossed the road. He was quite thrilled; this was only his second murder in thirty-one years as a Metropolitan Policeman, and it turned out to involve espionage! He might make Inspector yet.

He knocked on the door of number 42. It opened and two men stood there.

Sergeant Canter said: "Are you the secret agents from MI5?"

Bloggs arrived at the same time as a Special Branch man, Detective-Inspector Harris, whom he had known in his Scotland Yard days. Canter showed them the body.

They stood still for a moment, looking at the peaceful young face with its blond moustache.

Harris said, "Who is he?"

"Codename Blondie," Bloggs told him. "We think he came in by parachute a couple of weeks ago. We picked up a radio message to another agent arranging a rendezvous. We knew the code, so we were able to watch the rendezvous. We hoped Blondie would lead us to the resident agent, who would be a much more dangerous specimen."

"So what happened here?"

"Damned if I know."

Harris looked at the wound in the agent's chest. "Stiletto?"

"Something like that. A very neat job. Under the ribs and straight up into the heart. Quick. Would you like to see the method of entry?"

He led them downstairs to the kitchen. They looked at the windowframe and the unbroken pane of glass lying on the lawn.

Canter said, "Also, the lock on the bedroom door had been picked."

They sat down at the kitchen table, and Canter made tea. Bloggs said, "It happened the night after I lost him in Leicester Square. I fouled it all up."

Harris said, "Don't be so hard on yourself."

They drank their tea in silence for a while. Harris said, "How are things with you, anyway? You don't drop in at the Yard."

"Busy."

"How's Christine?"

"Killed in the bombing."

Harris's eyes widened. "You poor bastard."

"You all right?"

"Lost my brother in North Africa. Did you ever meet Johnny?"

"No."

"He was a lad. Drink? You've never seen anything like it. Spent so much on booze, he could never afford to get married—which is just as well, the way things turned out."

"Most have lost somebody, I guess."

"If you're on your own, come round our place for dinner on Sunday."

"Thanks, I work Sundays now."

Harris nodded. "Well, whenever you feel like it."

A detective-constable poked his head around the door and addressed Harris. "Can we start bagging-up the evidence, guv?"

Harris looked at Bloggs.

"I've finished," Bloggs said.

"All right, son, carry on," Harris told him.

Bloggs said, "Suppose he made contact after I lost him, and arranged for the resident agent to come here. The resident may have suspected a trap—that would explain why he came in through the window and picked the lock."

"It makes him a devilish suspicious bastard," Harris observed.

"That might be why we've never caught him. Anyway, he gets into Blondie's room and wakes him up. Now he knows it isn't a trap, right?"

"Right."

"So why does he kill Blondie?"

"Maybe they quarreled."

"There were no signs of a struggle."

Harris frowned into his empty cup. "Perhaps he realized that Blondie was being watched and he was afraid we'd pick the boy up and make him spill the beans."

Bloggs said, "That makes him a ruthless bastard."

"That, too, might be why we've never caught him."

"Come in. Sit down. I've just had a call from MI6. Canaris has been fired."

Bloggs went in, sat down, and said, "Is that good news or bad?"

"Very bad," said Godliman. "It's happened at the worst possible moment."

"Do I get told why?"

Godliman looked at him intently, then said, "I think you need to know. At this moment we have forty double agents broadcasting to Hamburg false information about Allied plans for the invasion of France."

Bloggs whistled. "I didn't know it was quite that big. I suppose the doubles say we're going in at Cherbourg, but really it will be Calais, or vice versa."

"Something like that. Apparently I don't need to know the details. Anyway they haven't told me. However, the whole thing is in danger. We knew Canaris; we knew we had him fooled; we felt we could have gone on fooling him. A new broom may mistrust his predecessor's agents. There's more—we've had some defections from the other side, people who could have betrayed the Abwehr's people over here if they hadn't been betrayed already. It's another reason for the Germans to begin to suspect our doubles.

"Then there's the possibility of a leak. Literally thousands of people now know about the double-cross system. There are doubles in Iceland, Canada, and Ceylon. We ran a double-cross in the Middle East.

"And we made a bad mistake last year by repatriating a German called Erich Carl. We later learned he was an Abwehr agent—a real one—and that while he was in internment on the Isle of Man he may have learned about two doubles, Mutt and Jeff, and possibly a third called Tate.

"So we're on thin ice. If one decent Abwehr agent in

Britain gets to know about Fortitude—that's the code name for the deception plan—the whole strategy will be endangered. Not to mince words, we could lose the fucking war."

Bloggs suppressed a smile—he could remember a time when Professor Godliman did not know the meaning of such words.

The professor went on, "The Twenty Committee has made it quite clear that they expect me to make sure there aren't any decent Abwehr agents in Britain."

"Last week we would have been quite confident that there weren't," Bloggs said.

"Now we know there's at least one."

"And we let him slip through our fingers."

"So now we have to find him again."

"I don't know," Bloggs said gloomily. "We don't know what part of the country he's operating from, we haven't the faintest idea what he looks like. He's too crafty to be pinpointed by triangulation while he's transmitting—otherwise we would have nabbed him long ago. We don't even know his code name. So where do we start?"

"Unsolved crimes," said Godliman. "Look—a spy is bound to break the law. He forges papers, he steals petrol and ammunition, he evades checkpoints, he enters restricted areas, he takes photographs, and when people rumble him he kills them. The police are bound to get to know of some of these crimes if the spy has been operating for any length of time. If we go through the unsolved crimes files since the war, we'll find traces."

"Don't you realize that *most* crimes are unsolved?" Bloggs said incredulously. "The files would fill the Albert Hall!"

Godliman shrugged. "So, we narrow it down to London, and we start with murders."

They found what they were looking for on the very first day of their search. It happened to be Godliman who came across it, and at first he did not realize its significance.

It was the file on the murder of a Mrs. Una Garden in Highgate in 1940. Her throat had been cut and she had been sexually molested, although not raped. She had been found in the bedroom of her lodger, with considerable alcohol in her bloodstream. The picture was fairly clear: she had had a tryst with the lodger, he had wanted to go farther than she was prepared to let him, they had quarreled, he had killed her, and the murder had neutralized his libido. But the police had never found the lodger.

Godliman had been about to pass over the file—spies did not get involved in sexual assaults. But he was a meticulous man with records, so he read every word, and consequently discovered that the unfortunate Mrs. Garden had received stiletto wounds in her back as well as the fatal wound to her throat.

Godliman and Bloggs were on opposite sides of a wooden table in the records room at Old Scotland Yard. Godliman tossed the file across the table and said, "I think this is it."

Bloggs glanced through it and said, "The stiletto."

They signed for the file and walked the short distance to the War Office. When they returned to Godliman's room, there was a decoded signal on his desk. He read it casually, then thumped the table in excitement. "It's him!"

Bloggs read: "Orders received. Regards to Willi."

"Remember him?" Godliman said. "Die Nadel?"

"Yes," Bloggs said hesitantly. "The Needle. But there's not much information here."

"Think, think! A stiletto is like a needle. It's the same man: the murder of Mrs. Garden, all those signals in 1940 that we couldn't trace, the rendezvous with Blondie . . ."

"Possibly." Bloggs looked thoughtful.

"I can prove it," Godliman said. "Remember the transmission about Finland that you showed me the first day I came here? The one that was interrupted?"

"Yes." Bloggs went to the file to find it.

"If my memory serves me well, the date of that trans-

mission is the same as the date of this murder . . . and I'll
bet the time of death coincides with the interruption."

Bloggs looked at the signal in the file. "Right both
times."

"There!"

"He's been operating in London for at least five years,
and it's taken us until now to get on to him," Bloggs reflected. "He won't be easy to catch."

Godliman suddenly looked wolfish. "He may be clever,
but he's not as clever as me," he said tightly. "I am going
to nail him to the fucking wall."

Bloggs laughed out loud. "My God, you've changed,
Professor."

Godliman said, "Do you realize that's the first time
you've laughed for a year?"

9

THE SUPPLY BOAT ROUNDED THE HEADLAND AND chugged into the bay at Storm Island under a blue sky.

There were two women in it: one was the skipper's wife—he had been called up and now she ran the business—and the other was Lucy's mother.

Mother got out of the boat wearing a utility suit, a mannish jacket and an above-the-knee skirt. Lucy hugged her mightily.

"Mother! What a surprise!"

"But I wrote to you."

The letter was with the mail on the boat; Mother had forgotten that the post only came once a fortnight on Storm Island.

"Is this my grandson? Isn't he a big boy?"

Little Jo, almost three years old, turned bashful and hid behind Lucy's skirt. He was dark-haired, pretty, and tall for his age.

Mother said: "Isn't he like his father!"

"Yes," Lucy said. "You must be freezing—come up to the house. Where *did* you get that skirt?"

They picked up the groceries and began to walk up the ramp to the cliff top. Mother chattered as they went. "It's the fashion, dear. It saves on material. But it isn't as cold as this on the mainland. Such a wind! I suppose it's all right to leave my case on the jetty—nobody to steal it! Jane is engaged to an American soldier—a white one, thank

God. He comes from a place called Milwaukee, and he doesn't chew gum. Isn't that nice? I've only got four more daughters to marry off now. Your father is a Captain in the Home Guard, did I tell you? He's up half the night patrolling the common waiting for German parachutists. Uncle Stephen's warehouse was bombed—I don't know *what* he'll do, it's an Act of War or something—"

"Don't rush, Mother, you've got fourteen days to tell me the news." Lucy laughed.

They reached the cottage. Mother said, "Isn't this *lovely*?" They went in. "I think this is just lovely."

Lucy parked Mother at the kitchen table and made tea. "Tom will get your case up. He'll be here for his lunch shortly."

"The shepherd?"

"Yes."

"Does he find things for David to do, then?"

Lucy laughed. "It's the other way around. I'm sure he'll tell you all about it himself. You haven't told me why you're here."

"My dear, it's about time I saw you. I know you're not supposed to make unnecessary journeys, but once in four years isn't extravagant, is it?"

They heard the jeep outside, and a moment later David wheeled himself in. He kissed his mother-in-law and introduced Tom.

Lucy said, "Tom, you can earn your lunch today by bringing Mother's case up, as she carried your groceries."

David was warming his hands at the stove. "It's raw today."

"You're really taking sheep-farming seriously, then?" Mother said.

"The flock is double what it was three years ago," David told her. "My father never farmed this island seriously. I've fenced six miles of the cliff top, improved the grazing, and introduced modern breeding methods. Not only do we have more sheep, but each animal gives us more meat and wool."

Mother said tentatively, "I suppose Tom does the physical work and you give the orders."

David laughed. "Equal partners, Mother."

They had hearts for lunch, and both men ate mountains of potatoes. Mother commented favorably on Jo's table manners. Afterwards David lit a cigarette and Tom stuffed his pipe.

Mother said, "What I really want to know is when you're going to give us more grandchildren." She smiled brightly.

There was a long silence.

"Well, I think it's wonderful, the way David copes," said Mother.

Lucy said, "Yes."

They were walking along the cliff top. The wind had dropped on the third day of Mother's visit and it was mild enough to go out. They took Jo, dressed in a fisherman's sweater and a fur coat. They had stopped at the top of a rise to watch David, Tom and the dog herding sheep. Lucy could see in Mother's face an internal struggle between concern and discretion. She decided to save her mother the effort of asking.

"He doesn't love me," she said.

Mother looked quickly to make sure Jo was out of earshot. "I'm sure it's not that bad, dear. Different men show their love in diff—"

"Mother, we haven't been man and wife—properly—since we were married."

"But? . . ." She indicated Jo with a nod.

"That was a week before the wedding."

"Oh! Oh, dear. Is it, you know, the accident?"

"Yes, but not in the way you mean. It's nothing physical. He just . . . won't." Lucy was crying quietly, the tears trickling down her wind-browned cheeks.

"Have you talked about it?"

"I've tried."

"Perhaps with time—"

"It's been almost four years!"

There was a pause. They began to walk on across the heather, into the weak afternoon sun. Jo chased gulls. Mother said, "I almost left your father, once."

It was Lucy's turn to be shocked. "When?"

"It was soon after Jane was born. We weren't so well-off in those days, you know—Father was still working for his father, and there was a slump. I was expecting for the third time in three years, and it seemed that a life of having babies and making ends meet stretched out in front of me with nothing to relieve the monotony. Then I discovered he was seeing an old flame of his—Brenda Simmonds, you never knew her, she went to Basingstoke. Suddenly I asked myself what I was doing it for, and I couldn't think of a sensible answer."

Lucy had dim, patchy memories of those days: her grandfather with a white moustache; her father in a more slender edition; extended family meals in the great farm-house kitchen; a lot of laughter and sunshine and animals. Even then her parents' marriage had seemed to represent solid contentment, happy permanence. She said, "Why didn't you? Leave, I mean."

"Oh, people just didn't, in those days. There wasn't all this divorce, and a woman couldn't get a job."

"Women work at all sorts of things now."

"They did in the last war, but everything changed afterward with a bit of unemployment. I expect it will be the same this time. Men get their way, you know, generally speaking."

"And you're glad you stayed." It was not a question.

"People my age shouldn't make pronouncements about life. But *my* life has been a matter of making-do, and the same goes for most of the women I know. Steadfastness always looks like a sacrifice, but usually it isn't. Anyway, I'm not going to give you advice. You wouldn't take it, and if you did you'd blame your problems on me, I expect."

"Oh, Mother." Lucy smiled.

Mother said, "Shall we turn around? I think we've gone far enough for one day."

In the kitchen one evening Lucy said to David, "I'd like Mother to stay another two weeks, if she will." Mother was upstairs putting Jo to bed, telling him a story.

"Isn't a fortnight long enough for you to dissect my personality?" David said.

"Don't be silly, David."

He wheeled himself over to her chair. "Are you telling me you don't talk about me?"

"Of course we talk about you—you're my husband."

"What do you say to her?"

"Why are you so worried?" Lucy said, not without malice. "What are you so ashamed of?"

"Damn you, I've nothing to be ashamed of. No one wants his personal life talked about by a pair of gossiping women—"

"We don't gossip about you."

"What do you say?"

"Aren't you touchy!"

"Answer my question."

"I say I want to leave you, and she tries to talk me out of it."

He spun around and wheeled away. "Tell her not to bother for my sake."

She called, "Do you mean that?"

He stopped. "I don't need anybody, do you understand? I can manage alone."

"And what about me?" she said quietly. "Perhaps I need somebody."

"What for?"

"To love me."

Mother came in, and sensed the atmosphere. "He's fast asleep," she said. "Dropped off before Cinderella got to the ball. I think I'll pack a few things, not to leave it all until tomorrow." She went out again.

"Do you think it will ever change, David?" Lucy asked.

"I don't know what you mean."

"Will we ever be . . . the way we were, before the wedding?"

"My legs won't grow back, if that's what you mean."

"Oh, God, don't you know that doesn't bother me? I just want to be loved."

David shrugged. "That's your problem." He went out before she started to cry.

Mother did not stay the second fortnight. Lucy walked with her down the jetty the next day. It was raining hard, and they both wore mackintoshes. They stood in silence waiting for the boat, watching the rain pit the sea with tiny craters. Mother held Jo in her arms.

"Things will change, in time, you know," she said. "Four years is nothing in a marriage."

Lucy said, "I don't know, but there's not much I can do. There's Jo, and the war, and David's condition—how *can* I leave?"

The boat arrived, and Lucy exchanged her mother for three boxes of groceries and five letters. The water was choppy. Mother sat in the boat's tiny cabin. They waved her around the headland. Lucy felt very lonely.

Jo began to cry. "I don't want Gran to go away!"

"Nor do I," said Lucy.

10

GODLIMAN AND BLOGGS WALKED SIDE BY SIDE along the pavement of a bomb-damaged London shopping street. They were a mismatched pair: the stooped, birdlike professor, with pebble-lensed spectacles and a pipe, not looking where he was going, taking short, scurrying steps; and the flat-footed youngster, blond and purposeful, in his detective's raincoat and melodramatic hat; a cartoon looking for a caption.

Godliman was saying, "I think Die Nadel is well-connected."

"Why?"

"The only way he could be so insubordinate with impunity. It's this 'Regards to Willi' line. It must refer to Canaris."

"You think he was pals with Canaris."

"He's pals with somebody—perhaps someone more powerful than Canaris was."

"I have the feeling this is leading somewhere."

"People who are well-connected generally make those connections at school, or university or staff college. Look at that."

They were outside a shop that had a huge empty space where once there had been a plate-glass window. A rough sign, hand-painted and nailed to the window-frame, said, "Even more open than usual."

Bloggs laughed, "I saw one outside a bombed police station: 'Be good, we are still open.' "

"It's become a minor art form."

They walked on. Bloggs said, "So, what if Die Nadel did go to school with someone high in the Wehrmacht?"

"People always have their pictures taken at school. Middleton down in the basement at Kensington—that house where MI6 used to be before the war—he's got a collection of thousands of photographs of German officers: school photos, binges in the Mess, passing-out parades, shaking hands with Adolf, newspaper pictures—everything."

"I see," Bloggs said. "So if you're right, and Die Nadel had been through Germany's equivalent of Eton and Sandhurst, we've probably got a picture of him."

"Almost certainly. Spies are notoriously camera-shy, but they don't become spies in school. It will be a youthful Die Nadel that we find in Middleton's files."

They skirted a huge crater outside a barber's. The shop was intact, but the traditional red-and-white-striped pole lay in shards on the pavement. The sign in the window said, "We've had a close shave—come and get one yourself."

"How will we recognize him? No one has ever seen him," Bloggs said.

"Yes, they have. At Mrs. Garden's boarding house in Highgate they know him quite well."

The Victorian house stood on a hill overlooking London. It was built of red brick, and Bloggs thought it looked angry at the damage Hitler was doing to its city. It was high up, a good place from which to broadcast. Die Nadel would have lived on the top floor. Bloggs wondered what secrets he had transmitted to Hamburg from this place in the dark days of 1940: map references for aircraft factories and steelworks, details of coastal defenses, political gossip, gas masks and Anderson shelters and sandbags, British morale, bomb damage reports, "Well done, boys, you got Christine Bloggs at last—" Shut up.

The door was opened by an elderly man in a black jacket and striped trousers.

"Good morning. I'm Inspector Bloggs, from Scotland Yard. I'd like a word with the householder, please."

Bloggs saw fear come to the man's eyes, then a young woman appeared in the doorway behind him and said, "Come in, please."

The tiled hall smelled of wax polish. Bloggs hung his hat and coat on a stand. The old man disappeared into the depths of the house, and the woman led Bloggs into a lounge. It was expensively furnished in a rich, old-fashioned way. There were bottles of whiskey, gin and sherry on a trolley; all the bottles were unopened. The woman sat on a floral arm-chair and crossed her legs.

"Why is the old man frightened of the police?" Bloggs said.

"My father-in-law is a German Jew. He came here in 1935 to escape Hitler, and in 1940 you put him in a concentration camp. His wife killed herself at the prospect. He has just been released from the Isle of Man. He had a letter from the King, apologizing for the inconvenience to which he had been put."

Bloggs said, "We don't have concentration camps."

"We invented them. In South Africa. Didn't you know? We go on about our history, but we forget bits. We're so good at blinding ourselves to unpleasant facts."

"Perhaps it's just as well."

"What?"

"In 1939 we blinded ourselves to the unpleasant fact that we alone couldn't win a war with Germany—and look what happened."

"That's what my father-in-law says. He's not as cynical as I. What can we do to assist Scotland Yard?"

Bloggs had been enjoying the debate, and now it was with reluctance that he turned his attention to work. "It's about a murder that took place here four years ago."

"So long!"

"Some new evidence may have come to light."

"I know about it, of course. The previous owner was

killed by a tenant. My husband bought the house from her executor—she had no heirs."

"I want to trace the other people who were tenants at that time."

"Yes." The woman's hostility had gone now, and her intelligent face showed the effort of recollection. "When we arrived there were three who had been here before the murder: a retired naval officer, a salesman and a young boy from Yorkshire. The boy joined the Army—he still writes to us. The salesman was called up and he died at sea. I know because two of his five wives got in touch with us! And the Commander is still here."

"Still here!" That was a piece of luck. "I'd like to see him, please."

"Surely." She stood up. "He's aged a lot. I'll take you to his room."

They went up the carpeted stairs to the first door. She said, "While you're talking to him, I'll look up the last letter from the boy in the Army." She knocked on the door. It was more than Bloggs's landlady would have done, he thought wryly.

A voice called, "It's open," and Bloggs went in.

The Commander sat in a chair by the window with a blanket over his knees. He wore a blazer, a collar and a tie, and spectacles. His hair was thin, his moustache grey, his skin loose and wrinkled over a face that might once have been strong. The room was the home of a man living on memories—there were paintings of sailing ships, a sextant and a telescope, and a photograph of himself as a boy aboard *HMS Winchester*.

"Look at this," he said without turning around. "Tell me why that chap isn't in the Navy."

Bloggs crossed to the window. A horse-drawn baker's van was at the curb outside the house, the elderly horse dipping into its nosebag while the deliveries were made. That "chap" was a woman with short blonde hair, in trousers. She had a magnificent bust. Bloggs laughed. "It's a woman in trousers," he said.

"Bless my soul, so it is!" The Commander turned around. "Can't tell these days, you know. Women in trousers!"

Bloggs introduced himself. "We've reopened the case of a murder committed here in 1940. I believe you lived here at the same time as the main suspect, one Henry Faber."

"Indeed! What can I do to help?"

"How well do you remember Faber?"

"Perfectly. Tall chap, dark hair, well-spoken, quiet. Rather shabby clothes—if you were the kind who judges by appearances, you might well mistake him. I didn't dislike him—wouldn't have minded getting to know him better, but he didn't want that. I suppose he was about your age."

Bloggs suppressed a smile—he was used to people assuming he must be older simply because he was a detective.

The Commander added, "I'm sure he didn't do it, you know. I know a bit about character—you can't command a ship without learning—and if that man was a sex maniac, I'm Hermann Goering."

Bloggs suddenly connected the blonde in trousers with the mistake about his age, and the conclusion depressed him. He said, "You know, you should always ask to see a policeman's warrant card."

The Commander was slightly taken aback. "All right, then, let's have it."

Bloggs opened his wallet and folded it to display the picture of Christine. "Here."

The Commander studied it for a moment, then said, "A very good likeness."

Bloggs sighed. The old man was very nearly blind.

He stood up. "That's all, for now," he said. "Thank you."

"Any time. Whatever I can do to help. I'm not much value to England these days—you've got to be pretty useless to get invalided out of the Home Guard, you know."

"Good-bye." Bloggs went out.

The woman was in the hall downstairs. She handed Bloggs a letter. "The boy's address is a Forces box number," she said. "Parkin's his name . . . no doubt you'll be able to find out where he is."

"You knew the Commander would be no use," Bloggs said.

"I guess not. But a visitor makes his day." She opened the door.

On impulse, Bloggs said, "Will you have dinner with me?"

A shadow crossed her face. "My husband is still on the Isle of Man."

"I'm sorry—I thought—"

"It's all right. I'm flattered."

"I wanted to convince you we're not the Gestapo."

"I know you're not. A woman alone just gets bitter."

Bloggs said, "I lost my wife in the bombing."

"Then you know how it makes you hate."

"Yes," said Bloggs. "It makes you hate." He went down the steps. The door closed behind him. It had started to rain. . . .

It had been raining then too. Bloggs was late home. He had been going over some new material with Godliman. Now he was hurrying, so that he would have half an hour with Christine before she went out to drive her ambulance. It was dark, and the raid had already started. The things Christine saw at night were so awful she had stopped talking about them.

Bloggs was proud of her, proud. The people she worked with said she was better than two men—she hurtled through blacked-out London, driving like a veteran, taking corners on two wheels, whistling and cracking jokes as the city turned to flame around her. Fearless, they called her. Bloggs knew better; she was terrified, but she would not let it show. He knew because he saw her eyes in the morning when he got up and she went to bed; when her guard was down and it was over for a few hours; he knew it was not fearlessness but courage, and he was proud.

It was raining harder when he got off the bus. He pulled down his hat and put up his collar. At a tobacconist's he bought cigarettes for Christine—she had started smoking recently like a lot of women. The shopkeeper would let him have only five, because of the storage. He put them in a Woolworth's bakelite cigarette case.

A policeman stopped him and asked for his identity card; another two minutes wasted. An ambulance passed him, similar to the one Christine drove; a requisitioned fruit truck, painted grey.

He began to get nervous as he approached home. The explosions were sounding closer, and he could hear the aircraft clearly. The East End was in for another bruising tonight; he would sleep in the Morrison shelter. There was a big one, terribly close, and he quickened his step. He would eat his supper in the shelter, too.

He turned into his own street, saw the ambulances and the fire engines, and broke into a run.

The bomb had landed on his side of the street, around the middle. It must be close to his own home. Jesus in heaven, not us, no—

There had been a direct hit on the roof, and the house was literally flattened. He raced up to the crowd of people, neighbors and firemen and volunteers. "Is my wife all right? Is she out? *Is she in there?*"

A fireman looked at him. "Nobody's come out of there, mate."

Rescuers were picking over the rubble. Suddenly one of them shouted, "Over here!" Then he said, "Jesus, it's Fearless Bloggs!"

Frederick dashed to where the man stood. Christine was underneath a huge chunk of brickwork. Her face was visible; the eyes were closed.

The rescuer called, "Lifting gear, boys, sharp's the word."

Christine moaned and stirred.

"She's alive!" Bloggs said. He knelt down beside her and got his hand under the edge of the lump of rubble.

The rescuer said, "You won't shift that, son."

The brickwork lifted.

"God, you'll kill yourself," the rescuer said, and bent down to help.

When it was two feet off the ground they got their shoulders under it. The weight was off Christine now. A third man joined in, and a fourth. They all straightened up together.

Bloggs said, "I'll lift her out."

He crawled under the sloping roof of brick and cradled his wife in his arms.

"Fuck me it's slipping!" someone shouted.

Bloggs scurried out from under with Christine held tightly to his chest. As soon as he was clear the rescuers let go of the rubble and jumped away. It fell back to earth with a sickening thud, and when Bloggs realized that *that* had landed on Christine, he knew she was going to die.

He carried her to the ambulance, and it took off immediately. She opened her eyes again once, before she died, and said, "You'll have to win the war without me, kiddo."

More than a year later, as he walked downhill from Highgate into the bowl of London, with the rain on his face mingling with the tears again, he thought the woman in the spy's house had said a mighty truth: It makes you hate.

In war boys become men and men become soldiers and soldiers get promoted; and this is why Bill Parkin, aged eighteen, late of a boarding house in Highgate, who should have been an apprentice in his father's tannery at Scarborough, was believed by the Army to be twenty-one, promoted to sergeant, and given the job of leading his advance squad through a hot, dry forest toward a dusty, whitewashed Italian village.

The Italians had surrendered but the Germans had not, and it was the Germans who were defending Italy against the combined British-American invasion. The Allies were going to Rome, and for Sergeant Parkin's squad it was a long walk.

They came out of the forest at the top of a hill, and lay flat on their bellies to look down on the village. Parkin got out his binoculars and said, "What wouldn't I fookin' give for a fookin' cup of fookin' tea." He had taken to drinking and cigarettes and women, and his language was like that of soldiers everywhere. He no longer went to prayer meetings.

Some of these villages were defended and some were not, Parkin recognized that as sound tactics—you didn't know which were undefended, so you approached them all cautiously, and caution cost time.

The downside of the hill held little cover—just a few bushes—and the village began at its foot. There were a few white houses, a river with a wooden bridge, then more houses around a little piazza with a town hall and a clock tower. There was a clear line of sight from the tower to the bridge; if the enemy were here at all, they would be in the town hall. A few figures worked in the surrounding fields; God knew who they were. They might be genuine peasants, or any one of a host of factions: fascisti, mafia, corsos, partigianos, communisti . . . or even Germans. You didn't know whose side they would be on until the shooting started.

Parkin said, "All right, Corporal."

Corporal Watkins disappeared back into the forest and emerged, five minutes later, on the dirt road into the village, wearing a civilian hat and a filthy old blanket over his uniform. He shambled, rather than walked, and over his shoulder was a bundle that could have been anything from a bag of onions to a dead rabbit. He reached the near edge of the village and vanished into the darkness of a low cottage.

After a moment he came out. Standing close to the wall, where he could not be seen from the village, he looked toward the soldiers on the hilltop and waved: one, two, three.

The squad scrambled down the hillside into the village.

"All the houses empty, Sarge," Watkins said.

Parkin nodded. It meant nothing.

They moved through the houses to the edge of the river. Parkin said, "Your turn, Smiler. Swim the Mississippi here."

Private "Smiler" Hudson put his equipment in a neat pile, took off his helmet, boots and tunic, and slid into the narrow stream. He emerged on the far side, climbed the bank, and disappeared among the houses. This time there was a longer wait: more area to check. Finally Hudson walked back across the wooden bridge. "If they're 'ere, they're 'iding," he said.

He retrieved his gear and the squad crossed the bridge into the village. They kept to the sides of the street as they walked toward the piazza. A bird flew off a roof and startled Parkin. Some of the men kicked open a few doors as they passed. There was nobody.

They stood at the edge of the piazza. Parkin nodded at the town hall. "Did you go inside that place, Smiler?"

"Yes, sir."

"Looks like the village is ours, then."

"Yes, sir."

Parkin stepped forward to cross the piazza, and then it broke. There was a crash of rifles, and bullets hailed all around them. Someone screamed. Parkin was running, dodging, ducking. Watkins, in front of him, shouted with pain and clutched his leg. Parkin picked him up bodily. A bullet clanged off his tin hat. He raced for the nearest house, charged the door, and fell inside.

The shooting stopped. Parkin risked a look outside. One man lay wounded in the piazza: Hudson. Hudson moved, and a solitary shot rang out. Then he was still. Parkin said, "Fookin' bastards."

Watkins was doing something to his leg, cursing. "Bullet still in there?" Parkin said.

Watkins yelled, "Ouch!" then grinned and held something up. "Not any more."

Parkin looked outside again. "They're in the clock tower. You wouldn't think there was room. Can't be many of them."

"They can shoot, though."

"Yes. They've got us pinned." Parkin frowned. "Got any fireworks?"

"Aye."

"Let's have a look." Parkin opened Watkins's pack and took out the dynamite. "Here. Fix a ten-second fuse."

The others were in the house across the street. Parkin called out "Hey!"

A face appeared at the door. "Sarge?"

"I'm going to throw a tomato. When I shout, give me covering fire."

"Right."

Parkin lit a cigarette. Watkins handed him a bundle of dynamite. Parkin shouted, "Fire!" He lit the fuse with the cigarette, stepped into the street, drew back his arm, and threw the bomb at the clock tower. He ducked back into the house, the fire of his own men ringing in his ears. A bullet shaved the woodwork, and he caught a splinter under his chin. He heard the dynamite explode.

Before he could look, someone across the street shouted, "Bullseye!"

Parkin stepped outside. The ancient clock tower had crumbled. A chime sounded incongruously as dust settled over the ruins.

Watkins said, "You ever play cricket? That was a bloody good shot."

Parkin walked to the center of the piazza. There seemed to be enough human spare parts to make about three Germans. "The tower was pretty unsteady anyway," he said. "It would probably have fallen down if we'd all sneezed at it together." He turned away. "Another day, another dollar." It was a phrase he'd heard the Yanks use.

"Sarge? Radio." It was the R/T operator.

Parkin walked back and took the handset from him. "Sergeant Parkin."

"Major Roberts. You're discharged from active duty as of now, Sergeant."

"Why?" Parkin's first thought was that they had discovered his true age.

"The brass want you in London. Don't ask me why because I don't know. Leave your corporal in charge and make your way back to base. A car will meet you on the road."

"Yes, sir."

"The orders also say that on no account are you to risk your life. Got that?"

Parkin grinned, thinking of the clock tower and the dynamite. "Got it."

"All right. On your way. You lucky sod."

Everyone had called him a boy, but they had known him before he joined the Army, Bloggs thought. There was no doubt he was a man now. He walked with confidence and grace, looked about him sharply, and was respectful without being ill at ease in the company of superior officers. Bloggs knew that he was lying about his age, not because of his looks or manner, but because of the small signs that appeared whenever age was mentioned—signs that Bloggs, an experienced interrogator, picked up out of habit.

He had been amused when they told him they wanted him to look at pictures. Now, in this third day in Mr. Middleton's dusty Kensington vault, the amusement had gone and tedium had set in. What irritated him most was the no-smoking rule.

It was even more boring for Bloggs, who had to sit and watch him.

At one point Parkin said, "You wouldn't call me back

from Italy to help you in a four-year-old murder case that could wait until after the war. Also, these pictures are mostly of German officers. If this case is something I should keep quiet about, you'd better tell me."

"It's something you should keep quiet about," said Bloggs.

Parkin went back to his pictures.

They were all old, mostly browned and fading. Many were out of books, magazines, and newspapers. Sometimes Parkin picked up a magnifying glass Mr. Middleton had thoughtfully provided, to peer more closely at a tiny face in a group; and each time this happened Bloggs's heart raced, only to slow down when Parkin put the glass to one side and picked up the next photograph.

They went to a nearby pub for lunch. The ale was weak, like most wartime beer, but Bloggs still thought it was wise to restrict young Parkin to two pints—on his own he would have sunk a gallon.

"Mr. Faber was the quiet sort," Parkin said. "You wouldn't think he had it in him. Mind you, the landlady wasn't bad looking. And she wanted it. Looking back, I think I could have had her myself if I'd known how to go about it. There, I was only—eighteen."

They ate bread and cheese, and Parkin swallowed a dozen pickled onions. When they went back, they stopped outside the house while Parkin smoked another cigarette.

"Mind you," he said, "he was a biggish chap, good-looking, well-spoken. We all thought he was nothing much because his clothes were poor, and he rode a bike, and he'd no money. I suppose it could have been a subtle kind of disguise." His eyebrows were raised in a question.

"It could have been," Bloggs said.

That afternoon Parkin found not one but three pictures of Faber. One of them was only nine years old.

And Mr. Middleton had the negative.

*　　*　　*

Heinrich Rudolph Hans von Müller-Güder (also known as Faber) was born on May 26, 1900, at a village called Oln in West Prussia. His father's family had been substantial landowners in the area for generations. His father was the second son; so was Heinrich. All the second sons were Army officers. His mother, the daughter of a senior official of the Second Reich, was born and raised to be an aristocrat's wife, and that was what she was.

At the age of thirteen Heinrich went to the Karlsruhe cadet school in Baden; two years later he was transferred to the more prestigious Gross-Lichterfelde, near Berlin. Both places were hard disciplinarian institutions where the minds of the pupils were improved with canes and cold baths and bad food. However, Heinrich learned to speak English and French and studied history, and passed the final examinations with the highest mark recorded since the turn of the century. There were only three other points of note in his school career: one bitter winter he rebelled against authority to the extent of sneaking out of the school at night and walking 150 miles to his aunt's house; he broke the arm of his wrestling instructor during a practice bout; and he was flogged for insubordination.

He served briefly as an ensign-cadet in the neutral zone of Friedrichsfeld, near Wesel, in 1920; did token officer training at the War School at Metz in 1921, and was commissioned Second Lieutenant in 1922.

("What was the phrase you used?" Godliman asked Bloggs. "The German equivalent of Eton and Sandhurst.")

Over the next few years he did short tours of duty in half a dozen places, in the manner of one who is being groomed for the general staff. He continued to distinguish himself as an athlete, specializing in long-distance running. He made no close friendships, never married, and refused to join the National Socialist party. His promotion to lieutenant was somewhat delayed by a vague incident involving the pregnancy of the daughter of a lieutenant colonel in the Defense Ministry, but eventually came about in 1928. His habit of talking to superior officers as if they were equals came to be accepted as pardonable in one who was both a rising young officer and a Prussian aristocrat.

In the late '20s Admiral Wilhelm Canaris became friendly with Heinrich's Uncle Otto, his father's elder brother, and spent several holidays at the family estate in Oln. In 1931 Adolf Hitler, not yet Chancellor of Germany, was a guest there.

In 1933 Heinrich was promoted to captain, and went to Berlin for unspecified duties. This is the date of the last photograph.

About then, according to published information, he seems to have ceased to exist. . . .

"We can conjecture the rest," said Percival Godliman. "The Abwehr trains him in wireless transmission, codes, map-making, burglary, blackmail, sabotage and silent killing. He comes to London in about 1937 with plenty of time to set himself up with a solid cover—perhaps two. His loner instincts are honed sharp by the spying game. When war breaks out, he considers himself licensed to kill." He looked at the photograph on his desk. "He's a handsome fellow."

It was a picture of the 5,000-meters running team of the 10th Hanoverian Jaeger Battalion. Faber was in the middle, holding a cup. He had a high forehead, with cropped hair, a long chin, and a small mouth decorated with a narrow moustache.

Godliman passed the picture to Billy Parkin. "Has he changed much?"

"He looked a lot older, but that might have been his . . . bearing." He studied the photograph thoughtfully. "His hair was longer, and the moustache was gone." He passed the picture back across the desk. "But it's him, all right."

"There are two more items in the file, both of them conjectural," Godliman said. "First, they say he may have gone into Intelligence in 1933—that's the routine assumption when an officer's record just stops for no apparent reason.

The second item is a rumor, unconfirmed by any reliable source, that he spent some years as a confidential advisor to Stalin, using the name Vasily Zankov."

"That's incredible," Bloggs said. "I don't believe that."

Godliman shrugged. "*Somebody* persuaded Stalin to execute the cream of his officer corps during the years Hitler rose to power."

Bloggs shook his head, and changed the subject. "Where do we go from here?"

Godliman considered. "Let's have Sergeant Parkin transferred to us. He's the only man we know who has actually seen Die Nadel. Besides, he knows too much for us to risk him in the front line; he could get captured and interrogated. Next, make a first-class print of this photo, and have the hair thickened and the moustache obliterated by a retouch artist. Then we can distribute copies."

"Do we want to start a hue and cry?" Bloggs said doubtfully.

"No. For now, let's tread softly. If we put the thing in the newspapers he'll get to hear of it and vanish. Just send the photo to police forces for the time being."

"Is that all?"

"I think so. Unless you've got other ideas."

Parkin cleared his throat. "Sir?"

"Yes."

"I really would prefer to go back to my unit. I'm not really the administrative type, if you see what I mean."

"You're not being offered a choice, Sergeant. At this stage, one Italian village more or less makes relatively little difference—but this man Faber could lose us the war. Truly."

11

FABER HAD GONE FISHING.

He was stretched out on the deck of a thirty-foot boat, enjoying the spring sunshine, moving along the canal at about three knots. One lazy hand held the tiller, the other rested on a rod that trailed its line in the water behind the boat.

He hadn't caught a thing all day.

As well as fishing, he was bird-watching—both out of interest (he was actually getting to know quite a lot about the damn birds) and as an excuse for carrying binoculars. Earlier today he had seen a kingfisher's nest.

The people at the boatyard in Norwich had been delighted to rent him the vessel for a fortnight. Business was bad—they had only two boats nowadays, and one of them had not been used since Dunkirk. Faber had haggled over the price, just for the sake of form. In the end they had thrown in a locker full of tinned food.

He had bought bait in a shop nearby; the fishing tackle he had brought from London. They had observed that he had nice weather for it, and wished him good fishing. Nobody asked to see his identity card.

So far, so good.

The difficult bit was to come. For assessing the strength of an army *was* difficult. First, for example, you had to find it.

In peacetime the Army would put up its own road signs

to help you. Now they had been taken down, not only the Army's but everyone else's road signs.

The simple solution would be to get in a car and follow the first military vehicle you saw until it stopped. However, Faber had no car; it was close to impossible for a civilian to hire one, and even if you got one you couldn't get petrol for it. Besides, a civilian driving around the countryside following Army vehicles and looking at Army camps was likely to be arrested.

Hence the boat.

Some years ago, before it had become illegal to sell maps, Faber had discovered that Britain had thousands of miles of inland waterways. The original network of rivers had been augmented during the nineteenth century by a spider web of canals. In some areas there was almost as much waterway as there was road. Norfolk was one of these areas.

The boat had many advantages. On a road, a man was going somewhere; on a river he was just sailing. Sleeping in a parked car was conspicuous; sleeping in a moored boat was natural. The waterway was lonely. And who ever heard of a canal-block?

There were disadvantages. Airfields and barracks had to be near roads, but they were located without reference to access by water. Faber had to explore the countryside at night, leaving his moored boat and tramping the hillsides by moonlight, exhausting forty-mile round trips during which he could easily miss what he was looking for because of the darkness or because he simply did not have enough time to check every square mile of land.

When he returned, a couple of hours after dawn, he would sleep until midday, then move on, stopping occasionally to climb a nearby hill and check the outlook. At locks, isolated farmhouses and riverside pubs he would talk to people, hoping for hints of a military presence. So far there had been none.

He was beginning to wonder whether he was in the right

area. He had tried to put himself in General Patton's place,
thinking: If I were planning to invade France east of the
Seine from a base in eastern England, where would I locate
that base? Norfolk was obvious: a vast expanse of lonely
countryside, plenty of flat ground for aircraft, close to the
sea for rapid departure. And the Wash was a natural place
to gather a fleet of ships. However, his guesswork might
be wrong for reasons unknown to him. Soon he would have
to consider a rapid move across country to a new area—
perhaps the Fens.

A lock appeared ahead of him, and he trimmed his sails
to slow his pace. He glided gently into the lock and bumped
softly against the gates. The lock-keeper's house was on
the bank. Faber cupped hands around his mouth and hal-
loed. Then he settled down to wait. He had learned that
lock-keepers were a breed that could not be hurried.
Moreover, it was tea time, and at tea time they could hardly
be moved at all.

A woman came to the door of the house and beckoned.
Faber waved back, then jumped onto the bank, tied up the
boat and went into the house. The lock-keeper was in his
shirtsleeves at the kitchen table. He said, "Not in a hurry,
are you?"

Faber smiled. "Not at all."

"Pour him a cup of tea, Mavis."

"No, really," Faber said politely.

"It's all right, we've just made a pot."

"Thank you." Faber sat down. The little kitchen was airy
and clean, and his tea came in a pretty china cup.

"Fishing holiday?" the lock-keeper asked.

"Fishing and bird-watching," Faber answered. "I'm
thinking of tying up quite soon and spending a couple of
days on land."

"Oh, aye. Well, best keep to the far side of the canal,
then. Restricted area this side."

"Really? I didn't know there was Army land here-
abouts."

"Aye, it starts about half a mile from here. As to whether it's Army, I wouldn't know. They don't tell me."

"Well, I suppose we don't need to know," Faber said.

"Aye. Drink up, then, and I'll see you through the lock. Thanks for letting me finish my tea."

They left the house, and Faber got into the boat and untied it. The gates behind him closed slowly, and then the keeper opened the sluices. The boat gradually sank with the level of the water in the lock, then the keeper opened the front gates.

Faber made sail and moved out. The lock-keeper waved.

He stopped again about four miles away and moored the boat to a stout tree on the bank. While he waited for night to fall he made a meal of tinned sausage meat, dry biscuits, and bottled water. He dressed in his black clothes, put into a shoulder bag his binoculars, camera, and copy of *Rare Birds of East Anglia*, pocketed his compass and picked up his flashlight. He was ready.

He doused the hurricane lamp, locked the cabin door and jumped onto the bank. Consulting his compass by flashlight, he entered the belt of woodland along the canal.

He walked due south from his boat for about half a mile until he came to the fence. It was six feet high, chicken wire, with coiled barbed wire on top. He backtracked into the wood and climbed a tall tree.

There was scattered cloud above. The moon showed through fitfully. Beyond the fence was open land, a gentle rise. Faber had done this sort of thing before, at Biggin Hill, Aldershot, and a host of military areas all over southern England. There were two levels of security: a mobile patrol around the perimeter fence, and stationary sentries at the installations.

Both, he felt, could be evaded by patience and caution.

Faber came down the tree and returned to the fence. He concealed himself behind a bush and settled down to wait.

He had to know when the mobile patrol passed this point. If they did not come until dawn he would simply return the following night. If he was lucky they would pass shortly. From the apparent size of the area under guard he guessed they would only make one complete tour of the fence each night.

He was lucky. Soon after ten o'clock he heard the tramp of feet, and three men marched by on the inside of the fence.

Five minutes later Faber crossed the fence.

He walked due south; when all directions are equal, a straight line is best. He did not use his flashlight. He kept close to hedges and trees when he could, and avoided high ground where he might be silhouetted against a sudden flash of moonlight. The sparse countryside was an abstract in black, grey and silver. The ground underfoot was a little soggy, as if there might be marshes nearby. A fox ran across a field in front of him, as fast as a greyhound, as graceful as a cat.

It was 11:30 P.M. when he came across the first indications of military activity—and very odd indications they were.

The moon came out and he saw, perhaps a quarter of a mile ahead, several rows of one-story buildings laid out with the unmistakable precision of an Army barracks. He dropped to the ground immediately, but he was already doubting the reality of what he apparently saw; for there were no lights and no noise.

He lay still for ten minutes, to give explanations a chance to emerge, but nothing happened except that a badger lumbered into view, saw him, and made off.

Faber crawled forward.

As he got closer he realized that the barracks were not just unoccupied, but unfinished. Most of them were little more than a roof supported by cornerposts. Some had one wall.

A sudden sound stopped him: a man's laugh. He lay still and watched. A match flared briefly and died, leaving two glowing red spots in one of the unfinished huts—guards.

Faber touched the stiletto in his sleeve, then began to crawl again, making for the side of the camp away from the sentries.

The half-built huts had no floors and no foundations. There were no construction vehicles around, no wheel-barrows, concrete mixers, shovels or piles of bricks. A mud track led away from the camp across the fields, but spring grass was growing in the ruts; it had not been used much lately.

It was as if someone had decided to billet 10,000 men here, then changed his mind a few weeks after building started.

Yet there was something about the place that did not quite fit that explanation.

Faber walked around softly, alert lest the sentries should take it into their heads to make a patrol. There was a group of military vehicles in the center of the camp. They were old and rusting, and had been degutted—none had an engine or any interior components. But if one was going to cannibalize obsolete vehicles, why not take the shells for scrap?

Those huts which did have a wall were on the outermost rows, and their walls faced out. It was like a movie set, not a building site.

Faber decided he had learned all he could from this place. He walked to the east edge of the camp, then dropped to his hands and knees and crawled away until he was out of sight behind a hedge. Half a mile farther on, near the top of a rise, he looked back. Now it looked exactly like a barracks again.

The glimmer of an idea formed in his mind. He gave it time.

The land was still relatively flat, relieved only by gentle folds. There were patches of woodland and marshy scrub that Faber took advantage of. Once he had to detour around a lake, its surface a silver mirror under the moon. He heard the hoot of an owl, and looked in that direction to see a tumbledown barn in the distance.

Five miles on he saw the airfield.

There were more planes here than he thought were possessed by the entire Royal Air Force. There were Pathfinders to drop flares, Lancasters and American B-17s for softening-up bombing, Hurricanes and Spitfires and Mosquitoes for reconnaissance and strafing; enough planes for an invasion.

Without exception their undercarriages had sunk into the soft earth and they were up to their bellies in mud.

Once again there were no lights and no noise.

Faber followed the same procedure, crawling flat toward the planes until he located the guards. In the middle of the airfield was a small tent. The faint glow of a lamp shone through the canvas. Two men, perhaps three.

As Faber approached the planes they seemed to become flatter, as if they had all been squashed.

He reached the nearest and touched it in amazement. It was a piece of half-inch plywood, cut out in the outline of a Spitfire, painted with camouflage, and roped to the ground.

Every other plane was the same.

There were more than a thousand of them.

Faber got to his feet, watching the tent from the corner of his eye, ready to drop to the ground at the slightest sign of movement. He walked all around the phony airfield, looking at the phony fighters and bombers, connecting them with the movie-set barracks, reeling at the implications of what he had found.

He knew that if he continued to explore he would find more airfields like this, more half-built barracks. If he went to the Wash he would find a fleet of plywood destroyers and troop ships.

It was a vast, meticulous, costly, outrageous trick.

Of course it could not possibly fool an onlooker for very

long. But it was not designed to deceive observers on the ground.

It was meant to be seen from the air.

Even a low-flying reconnaissance plane equipped with the latest cameras and fast film would come back with pictures that indisputably showed an enormous concentration of men and machines.

No wonder the general staff was anticipating an invasion east of the Seine.

There would be other elements to the deception, he guessed. The British would refer to FUSAG in signals, using codes they knew to be broken. There would be phony espionage reports channeled through the Spanish diplomatic bag to Hamburg. The possibilities were endless.

The British had had four years to arm themselves for this invasion. Most of the German army was fighting Russia. Once the Allies got a toehold on French soil they would be unstoppable. The Germans' only chance was to catch them on the beaches and annihilate them as they came off the troop ships.

If they were waiting in the wrong place, they would lose that one chance.

The whole strategy was immediately clear. It was simple, and it was devastating.

Faber had to tell Hamburg.

He wondered whether they would believe him.

War strategy was rarely altered on the word of one man. His own standing was high, but was it *that* high?

That idiot Von Braun would never believe him. He'd hated Faber for years and would grab at the opportunity to discredit him. Canaris, Von Roenne . . . he had no faith in them.

And there was another thing: the radio. He didn't want to trust this to the radio . . . he'd had the feeling for weeks now that the radio code wasn't safe anymore. If the British found out that their secret was blown . . .

There was only one thing to do: he had to get proof, and he had to take it himself to Berlin.

He needed photographs.

He would take photographs of this gigantic dummy army, then he would go to Scotland and meet the U-boat, and he would deliver the pictures personally to the Fuehrer. He could do no more. No less.

For photography he needed light. He would have to wait until dawn. There had been a ruined barn a little way back—he could spend the rest of the night there.

He checked his compass and set off. The barn was farther than he thought, and the walk took him an hour. It was an old wooden building with holes in the roof. The rats had long ago deserted it for lack of food, but there were bats in the hayloft.

Faber lay down on some planks but he could not sleep. Not with the knowledge that he was now personally capable of altering the course of the war.

Dawn was due at 05:21. At 04:20 Faber left the barn.

Although he had not slept, the two hours had rested his body and calmed his mind, and he was now in fine spirits. The cloud was clearing with a west wind, so although the moon had set there was starlight.

His timing was good. The sky was growing perceptibly brighter as he came in sight of the "airfield."

The sentries were still in their tent. With luck, they would be sleeping. Faber knew from his own experience of such duties that it was hardest to stay awake during the last few hours.

But if they did come out, he would have to kill them.

He selected his position and loaded the Leica with a 36-frame roll of 35mm fast Agfa film. He hoped the film's light-sensitive chemicals had not spoiled; it had been stored in his suitcase since before the war, and you couldn't buy film in Britain nowadays. It should be all right; he had kept it in a lightproof bag away from any heat.

When the red rim of the sun edged over the horizon he began shooting. He took a series of shots from different vantage points and various distances, finishing with a close-up of one dummy plane; the pictures would show both the illusion and the reality.

As he took the last, he saw movement from the corner of his eye. He dropped flat and crawled under a plywood Mosquito. A soldier emerged from the tent, walked a few paces, and urinated on the ground. The man stretched and yawned, then lit a cigarette. He looked around the airfield, shivered, and returned to the tent.

Faber got up and ran.

A quarter of a mile away he looked back. The airfield was out of sight. He headed west, toward the barracks.

This would be more than an ordinary espionage coup. Hitler had had a life of being the only one in step. The man who brought the proof that, yet again, the Fuehrer was right and all the experts were wrong, could look for more than a pat on the back. Faber knew that already Hitler rated him the Abwehr's best agent—this triumph might well get him Canaris's job.

If he made it.

He increased his pace, jogging twenty yards, walking the next twenty, and jogging again, so that he reached the barracks by 06:30. It was bright daylight now, and he could not approach close because these sentries were not in a tent but in one of the wall-less huts with a clear view all around them. He lay down by the hedge and took his pictures from a distance. Ordinary prints would just show a barracks, but big enlargements ought to reveal the details of the deception.

When he headed back toward the boat he had exposed thirty frames. Again he hurried, because he was now terribly conspicuous, a black-clad man carrying a canvas bag of equipment, jogging across the open fields of a restricted area.

He reached the fence an hour later, having seen nothing

but wild geese. As he climbed over the wire, he felt a great release of tension. Inside the fence the balance of suspicion had been against him; outside it was in his favor. He could revert to his bird-watching, fishing, sailing role. The period of greatest risk was over.

He strolled through the belt of woodland, catching his breath and letting the strain of the night's work seep away. He would sail a few miles on, he decided, before mooring again to catch a few hours' sleep.

He reached the canal. It was over. The boat looked pretty in the morning sunshine. As soon as he was under way he would make some tea, then—

A man in uniform stepped out of the cabin of the boat and said: "Well, well. And who might you be?"

Faber stood still, letting the icy calm and the old instincts come into play. The intruder wore the uniform of a captain in the Home Guard. He had some kind of handgun in a holster with a buttoned flap. He was tall and rangy, but he looked to be in his late fifties. White hair showed under his cap. He made no move to draw his gun. Faber took all this in as he said, "You are on my boat, so I think it is I who should ask who you are."

"Captain Stephen Langham, Home Guard."

"James Baker." Faber stayed on the bank. A captain did not patrol alone.

"And what are you doing?"

"I'm on holiday."

"Where have you been?"

"Bird-watching."

"Since before dawn? Cover him, Watson."

A youngish man in denim uniform appeared on Faber's left, carrying a shotgun. Faber looked around. There was another man to his right and a fourth behind him.

The captain called, "Which direction did he come from, corporal?"

The reply came from the top of an oak tree. "From the restricted area, sir."

Faber was calculating odds. Four to one—until the corporal came down from the tree. They had only two guns, the shotgun and the captain's pistol. And they were basically amateurs. The boat would help too.

He said, "Restricted area? All I saw was a bit of fence. Look, do you mind pointing that blunderbuss away? It might go off."

"Nobody goes bird-watching in the dark," the captain said.

"If you set up your hide under cover of darkness, you're concealed by the time the birds wake up. It's the accepted way to do it. Now look, the Home Guard is jolly patriotic and keen and all that, but let's not take it too far. Don't you just have to check my papers and file a report?"

The captain was looking a shade doubtful. "What's in that canvas bag?"

"Binoculars, a camera, and a reference book." Faber's hand went to the bag.

"No, you don't," the captain said. "Look inside it, Watson."

There it was—the amateur's error.

Watson said, "Raise your hands."

Faber raised his hands above his head, his right hand close to the left sleeve of his jacket. Faber choreographed the next few seconds—there must be no gunfire.

Watson came up on Faber's left side, pointing the shotgun at him, and opened the flap of Faber's canvas bag. Faber drew the stiletto from his sleeve, moved inside Watson's guard, and plunged the knife into Watson's neck up to the hilt. Faber's other hand twisted the shotgun out of the young man's grasp.

The other two soldiers on the bank moved toward him, and the corporal began to crash down through the branches of the oak.

Faber tugged the stiletto out of Watson's neck as the man collapsed to the ground. The captain was fumbling at the flap of his holster. Faber leaped into the well of the boat.

It rocked, sending the captain staggering. Faber struck at him with the knife, but the man was too far away for an accurate thrust. The point caught in the lapel of his uniform jacket, then jerked up, slashing his chin. His hand came away from the holster to clutch the wound.

Faber whipped around to face the bank. One of the soldiers jumped. Faber stepped forward and held his right arm out rigidly. The leaping soldier impaled himself on the eight-inch stiletto.

The impact knocked Faber off his feet, and he lost his grip on the stiletto. The soldier fell on top of the weapon. Faber got to his knees; there was no time to retrieve the stiletto, the captain was opening his holster. Faber jumped at him, his hands going for the officer's face. The gun came out. Faber's thumbs gouged at the eyes of the captain, who screamed in pain and tried to push Faber's arms aside.

There was a thud as the fourth guardsman landed in the well of the boat. Faber turned from the captain, who would now be unable to see to fire his pistol even if he could get the safety off. The fourth man held a policeman's truncheon; he brought it down hard. Faber shifted to the right so that the blow missed his head and caught his left shoulder. His left arm momentarily went nerveless. He chopped the man's neck with the side of his hand, a powerful, accurate blow. Amazingly the man survived it and brought his truncheon up for a second swipe. Faber closed in. The feeling returned to his left arm, and it began to hurt mightily. He took the soldier's face in both his hands, pushed, twisted, and pushed again. There was a sharp crack as the man's neck broke. At the same instant the truncheon landed again, this time on Faber's head. He reeled away, dazed.

The captain bumped into him, still staggering. Faber pushed him. His cap went flying as he stumbled backward over the gunwale and fell into the canal with a huge splash.

The corporal jumped the last six feet from the oak tree onto the ground. Faber retrieved his stiletto from the impaled guard and leaped to the bank. Watson was still alive, but it would not be for long—blood was pumping out of the wound in his neck.

Faber and the corporal faced each other. The corporal had a gun.

He was understandably terrified. In the seconds it had taken him to climb down the oak tree this man had killed three of his mates and thrown the fourth into the canal.

Faber looked at the gun. It was *old*—almost like a museum piece. If the corporal had any confidence in it, he would already have fired it.

The corporal took a step forward, and Faber noticed that he favored his right leg—perhaps he had hurt it coming out of the tree. Faber stepped sideways, forcing the corporal to put his weight on the weak leg as he swung to keep his gun on the target. Faber got the toe of his shoe under a stone and kicked upward. The corporal's attention flicked to the stone, and Faber moved.

The corporal pulled the trigger; nothing happened. The old gun had jammed. Even if it had fired, he would have missed Faber; his eyes were on the stone, he stumbled on the weak leg, and Faber had moved.

Faber killed him with the neck stab.

Only the captain was left.

Faber looked, and saw the man clambering out of the water on the far bank. He found a stone and threw it. It hit the captain's head, but the man heaved himself onto dry land and began to run.

Faber ran to the bank, dived in, swam a few strokes, and came up on the far side. The captain was a hundred yards away and running, but he was old. Faber gained steadily until he could hear the man's agonized, ragged breathing. The captain slowed, then collapsed into a bush. Faber came up to him and turned him over.

The captain said, "You're a . . . devil."

"You saw my face," Faber said, and killed him.

12

THE JU-52 TRIMOTOR TRANSPORT PLANE WITH swastikas on the wings bumped to a halt on the rain-wet runway at Rastenburg in the East Prussian forest. A small man with big features—a large nose, a wide mouth, big ears—disembarked and walked quickly across the tarmac to a waiting Mercedes car.

As the car drove through the gloomy, damp forest, Field Marshal Erwin Rommel took off his cap and rubbed a nervous hand along his receding hairline. In a few weeks' time, he knew, another man would travel this route with a bomb in his briefcase—a bomb destined for the Fuehrer himself. Meanwhile the fight must go on, so that the new leader of Germany—who might even be himself—could negotiate with the Allies from a reasonably strong position.

At the end of a ten-mile drive the car arrived at the Wolfsschanze, the Wolves' Lair, headquarters now for Hitler and the increasingly tight, neurotic circle of generals who surrounded him.

There was a steady drizzle, and raindrops dripped from the tall conifers in the compound. At the gate to Hitler's personal quarters, Rommel put on his cap and got out of the car. Oberfuehrer Rattenhuber, the chief of the SS bodyguard, wordlessly held out his hand to receive Rommel's pistol.

The conference was to be held in the underground bunker, a cold, damp, airless shelter lined with concrete. Rommel went down the steps and entered. There were a dozen or so there already, waiting for the noon meeting: Himmler, Goering, von Ribbentrop, Keitel. Rommel nodded greetings and sat on a hard chair to wait.

They all stood when Hitler entered. He wore a grey tunic and black trousers, and, Rommel observed, he was becoming increasingly stooped. He walked straight to the far end of the bunker, where a large wall map of northwestern Europe was tacked to the concrete. He looked tired and irritable. He spoke without preamble.

"There will be an Allied invasion of Europe. It will come this year. It will be launched from Britain, with English and American troops. They will land in France. We will destroy them at the high-water mark. On this there is no room for discussion."

He looked around, as if daring his staff to contradict him. There was silence. Rommel shivered; the bunker was as cold as death.

"The question is, where will they land? Von Roenne—your report."

Colonel Alexis von Roenne, who had taken over, effectively, from Canaris, got to his feet. A mere captain at the outbreak of war, he had distinguished himself with a superb report on the weakness of the French army—a report that had been called a decisive factor in the German victory. He had become chief of the army intelligence bureau in 1942, and that bureau had absorbed the Abwehr on the fall of Canaris. Rommel had heard that he was proud and outspoken, but able.

Von Roenne said, "Our information is extensive, but by no means complete. The Allies' code name for the invasion is Overlord. Troop concentrations in Britain are as follows." He picked up a pointer and crossed the room to the wall map. "First: along the south coast. Second: here in the district known as East Anglia. Third: in Scotland. The East Anglian concentration is *by far* the greatest. We conclude that the invasion will be three-pronged. First: a diversionary attack on Normandy. Second: the main thrust, across the Strait of Dover to the Calais coast. Third: a flanking invasion from Scotland across the North Sea to Norway. All intelligence sources support this prognosis." He sat down.

Hitler said, "Comments?"

Rommel, who was Commander of Army Group B, which controlled the north coast of France, said, "I can report one confirming sign: the Pas de Calais has received by far the greatest tonnage of bombs."

Goering said, "What intelligence sources support your prognosis, Von Roenne?"

Von Roenne stood up again. "There are three: air reconnaissance, monitoring of enemy wireless signals and the reports of agents." He sat down.

Hitler crossed his hands protectively in front of his genitals, a nervous habit that was a sign that he was about to make a speech. "I shall now tell you," he began, "how I would be thinking if I were Winston Churchill. Two choices confront me: east of the Seine, or west of the Seine. East has one advantage: it is nearer. But in modern warfare there are only two distances—*within* fighter range and *outside* fighter range. *Both* of these choices are within fighter range. Therefore distance is not a consideration.

"West has a great port—Cherbourg—but east has none. And most important—east is more heavily fortified than west. The enemy too has air reconnaissance.

"So, I would choose west. And what would I do then? I would try to make the Germans think the opposite! I would send two bombers to the Pas de Calais for every one to Normandy. I would try to knock out every bridge over the Seine. I would put out misleading wireless signals, send false intelligence reports, dispose my troops in a misleading fashion. I would deceive fools like Rommel and von Roenne. I would hope to deceive the Fuehrer himself!"

Goering spoke first after a lengthy silence. "My Fuehrer, I believe you flatter Churchill by crediting him with ingenuity equal to your own."

There was a noticeable easing of tension in the uncomfortable bunker. Goering had said exactly the right thing, managing to voice his disagreement in the form of a compliment. The others followed him, each stating the case a little more strongly—the Allies would choose the shorter sea crossing for speed; the closer coast would allow the covering fighter aircraft to refuel and return in shorter time; the southeast was a better launch pad, with more estuaries and harbors; it was unlikely that *all* the intelligence reports would be wrong.

Hitler listened for half an hour, then held up his hands for silence. He picked up a yellowing sheaf of papers from the table and waved them. "In 1941," he said, "I issued my directive *Construction of Coastal Defenses*, in which I forecast that the decisive landing of the Allies would come at the protruding parts of Normandy and Brittany, where the excellent harbors would make ideal beachheads. That was what my intuition told me then, and that is what it tells me now!" A fleck of foam appeared on the Fuehrer's lower lip.

Von Roenne spoke up. (He has more courage than I, Rommel thought.) "My Fuehrer, our investigations continue, quite naturally, and there is one particular line of inquiry that you should know about. I have in recent weeks sent an emissary to England to contact the agent known as Die Nadel."

Hitler's eyes gleamed. "Ah! I know the man. Go on."

"Die Nadel's orders are to assess the strength of the First United States Army Group under General Patton in East Anglia. If he finds that this has been exaggerated, we must surely reconsider our prognosis. If, however, he reports that the army is as strong as we presently believe, there can be little doubt that Calais is the target."

Goering looked at von Roenne. "Who is this Nadel?"

Hitler answered the question. "The only decent agent Canaris ever recruited—because he recruited him at my direction. I know his family—strong, loyal, upright Germans.

And Die Nadel—a brilliant man, brilliant! I see all his reports. He has been in London since—"

Von Roenne interrupted: "My Fuehrer—"

Hitler glared at him. "Well?"

Von Roenne said tentatively, "Then you will accept Die Nadel's report?"

Hitler nodded. "That man will discover the truth."

PART
THREE

13

FABER LEANED AGAINST A TREE, SHIVERING, AND threw up. Then he considered whether he should bury the five dead men.

It would take between thirty and sixty minutes, he estimated, depending on how well he concealed the bodies. During that time he might be caught.

He had to weigh that risk against the precious hours he might gain by delaying the discovery of the deaths. The five men would be missed very soon—there would be a search under way by around nine o'clock. Assuming they were on a regular patrol, their route would be known. The searchers' first move would be to send a runner to cover the route. If the bodies were left as they were, he would see them and raise the alarm. Otherwise, he would report back and a full-scale search would be mounted, with bloodhounds and policemen beating the bushes. It might take them all day to discover the corpses. By that time Faber could be in London. It was important for him to be out of the area before they knew they were looking for a murderer. He decided to risk the additional hour.

He swam back across the canal with the elderly captain across his shoulder, dumped him unceremoniously behind a bush, then retrieved the two bodies from the well of the boat and piled them on top of the captain. Next he added Watson and the corporal to the heap.

He had no spade and he needed a big grave. He found

a patch of loose earth a few yards into the wood. The ground there was slightly hollowed, to give him an advantage. He got a saucepan from the boat's tiny galley and began to dig.

For a couple of feet there was just leaf mold, and the going was easy. Then he got down to clay and digging became extremely difficult. In half an hour he had added only another eighteen inches of depth to the hole. It would have to do.

He carried the bodies to the hole one by one and threw them in. Then he took off his muddy, bloodstained clothes and dropped them on top. He covered the grave with loose earth and a layer of foliage ripped from nearby bushes and trees. It should be good enough to pass that first superficial inspection.

He kicked earth over the patch of ground near the bank where the life-blood of Watson had poured out. There was blood in the boat, too, where the impaled soldier had lain. Faber found a rag and swabbed down the deck.

Then he put on clean clothes, made sail, and moved off.

He did not fish or watch birds; this was no time for pleasant embellishments to his cover. Instead he piled on the sail, putting as much distance as possible between himself and the grave. He had to get off the water and into some faster transport as soon as possible. He reflected, as he sailed, on the relative merits of catching a train and stealing a car. A car was faster, if one could be found to steal; but the search for it might start quite soon, regardless of whether the theft was connected with the missing Home Guard patrol. Finding a railway station might take a long time, but it seemed safer; if he were careful he could escape suspicion for most of the day.

He wondered what to do about the boat. Ideally he would scuttle it, but he might be seen doing so. If he left it in a harbor somewhere, or simply moored at the canalside, the police would connect it with the murders that much sooner;

and that would tell them in which direction he was moving. He postponed the decision.

Unfortunately, he was not sure where he was. His map of England's waterways gave every bridge, harbor and lock; but it did not show railway lines. He calculated he was within an hour or two's walk of half a dozen villages, but a village did not necessarily mean a station.

The two problems were solved at once; the canal went under a railway bridge.

He took his compass, the film from the camera, his wallet and his stiletto. All his other possessions would go down with the boat.

The towpath on both sides was shaded with trees, and there were no roads nearby. He furled the sails, dismantled the base of the mast, and laid the pole on the deck. Then he removed the bung-hole stopper from the keel and stepped on to the bank, holding the rope.

Gradually filling with water, the boat drifted under the bridge. Faber hauled on the rope to hold the vessel in position directly under the brick arch as it sank. The afterdeck went under first, the prow followed, and finally the water of the canal closed over the roof of the cabin. There were a few bubbles, then nothing. The outline of the boat was hidden from a casual glance by the shadow of the bridge. Faber threw the rope in.

The railway line ran northeast to southwest. Faber climbed the embankment and walked southwest, which was the direction in which London lay. It was a two-line track, probably a rural branch line. There would be a few trains, but they would stop at all stations.

The sun grew stronger as he walked, and the exertion made him hot. When he had buried his bloodstained black clothes he had put on a double-breasted blazer and heavy flannel trousers. Now he took off the blazer and slung it over his shoulder.

After forty minutes he heard a distant chuff-chuff-chuff and hid in a bush beside the line. An old steam engine went slowly by, heading northeast, puffing great clouds of smoke and hauling a train of coal trucks. If one came by in the opposite direction, he could jump it. Should he? It would save him a long walk. On the other hand, he would get conspicuously dirty and he might have trouble disembarking without being seen. No, it was safer to walk.

The line ran straight as an arrow across the flat countryside. Faber passed a farmer, ploughing a field with a tractor. There was no way to avoid being seen. The farmer waved to him without stopping in his work. He was too far away to get a good sight of Faber's face.

He had walked about ten miles when he saw a station ahead. It was half a mile away, and all he could see was the rise of the platforms and a cluster of signals. He left the line and cut across the fields, keeping close to borders of trees, until he met a road.

Within a few minutes he entered the village. There was nothing to tell him its name. Now that the threat of invasion was a memory, sign-posts and place-names were being re-erected, but this village had not got around to it.

There was a Post Office, a Corn Store, and a pub called The Bull. A woman with a pram gave him a friendly "Good morning!" as he passed the War Memorial. The little station basked sleepily in the spring sunshine. Faber went in.

A timetable was pasted to a notice-board. Faber stood in front of it. From behind the little ticket window a voice said: "I shouldn't take any notice of that, if I were you. It's the biggest work of fiction since *The Forsyte Saga*."

Faber had known the timetable would be out of date, but he had needed to establish whether the trains went to London. They did. He said, "Any idea what time the next train leaves for Liverpool Street?"

The clerk laughed sarcastically. "Sometime today, if you're lucky."

"I'll buy a ticket anyway. Single, please."

"Five-and-fourpence. They say the Italian trains run on time," the clerk said.

"Not anymore," Faber remarked. "Anyway, I'd rather have bad trains and our politics."

The man shot him a nervous look. "You're right, of course. Do you want to wait in The Bull? You'll hear the train—or, if not, I'll send for you."

Faber did not want more people to see his face. "No, thanks, I'd only spend money." He took his ticket and went on to the platform.

The clerk followed him a few minutes later, and sat on the bench beside him in the sunshine. He said, "You in a hurry?"

Faber shook his head. "I've written today off. I got up late, I quarreled with the boss, and the truck that gave me a lift broke down."

"One of those days. Ah, well." The clerk looked at his watch. "She went up on time this morning, and what goes up must come down, they say. You might be lucky." He went back into his office.

Faber was lucky. The train came twenty minutes later. It was crowded with farmers, families, businessmen and soldiers. Faber found a space on the floor close to a window. As the train lumbered away, he picked up a discarded two-day-old newspaper, borrowed a pencil, and started to do the crossword. He was proud of his ability to do crosswords in English—it was the acid test of fluency in a foreign language. After a while the motion of the train lulled him into a shallow sleep, and he dreamed.

It was a familiar dream, the dream of his arrival in London.

He had crossed from France, carrying a Belgian passport that said he was Jan van Gelder, a representative for Phillips (which would explain his suitcase radio if Customs opened it). His English then was fluent but not colloquial. The Customs had not bothered him; he was an ally. He had caught the train to London. In those days there had been plenty of empty seats in the carriages, and you could get a meal. Faber had dined on roast beef and Yorkshire pudding.

It amused him. He had talked with a history student from Cardiff about the European political situation. The dream was like the reality until the train stopped at Waterloo. Then it turned into a nightmare.

The trouble started at the ticket barrier. Like all dreams it had its own weird illogicality. The document they queried was not his forged passport but his perfectly legitimate railway ticket. The collector said, "This is an Abwehr ticket."

"No, it is not," said Faber, speaking with a ludicrously thick German accent. What had happened to his dainty English consonants? They would not come. "I have it in Dover gekauft." Damn, that did it.

But the ticket collector, who had turned into a London policeman complete with helmet, seemed to ignore the sudden lapse into German. He smiled politely and said, "I'd better just check your Klamotte, sir."

The station was crowded with people. Faber thought that if he could get into the crowd he might escape. He dropped the suitcase radio and fled, pushing his way through the crowd. Suddenly he realized he had left his trousers on the train, and there were swastikas on his socks. He would have to buy trousers at the very first shop, before people noticed the trouserless running man with Nazi hose. Then someone in the crowd said, "I've seen your face before," and tripped him, and he fell with a bump and landed on the floor of the railway carriage where he had gone to sleep.

He blinked, yawned and looked around him. He had a headache. For a moment he was filled with relief that it was all a dream, then he was amused by the ridiculousness of the symbolism—swastika socks, for God's sake!

A man in overalls beside him said, "You had a good sleep."

Faber looked up sharply. He was always afraid of talking in his sleep and giving himself away. "I had an unpleasant dream," he said. The man made no comment.

It was getting dark. He *had* slept for a long time. The

carriage light came on suddenly, a single blue bulb, and someone drew the blinds. People's faces turned into pale, featureless ovals. The workman became talkative again. "You missed the excitement," he told Faber.

Faber frowned. "What happened?" It was impossible he should have slept through some kind of police check.

"One of them Yank trains passed us. It was going about ten miles an hour, nigger driving it, ringing its bell, with a bloody great cowcatcher on the front! Talk about the Wild West."

Faber smiled and thought back to the dream. In fact his arrival in London had been without incident. He had checked into a hotel at first, still using his Belgian cover. Within a week he had visited several country churchyards, taken the names of men his age from the gravestones, and applied for three duplicate birth certificates. Then he took lodgings and found humble work, using forged references from a nonexistent Manchester firm. He had even got on to the electoral register in Highgate before the war. He voted Conservative. When rationing came in, the ration books were issued via householders to every person who had slept in the house on a particular night. Faber contrived to spend part of that night in each of three different houses, and so obtained papers for each of his personae. He burned the Belgian passport—in the unlikely event he should need a passport, he could get three British ones.

The train stopped, and from the noise outside the passengers guessed they had arrived. When Faber got out he realized how hungry and thirsty he was. His last meal had been sausage-meat, dry biscuits and bottled water, twenty-four hours ago. He went through the ticket barrier and found the station buffet. It was full of people, mostly soldiers, sleeping or trying to sleep at the tables. Faber asked for a cheese sandwich and a cup of tea.

"The food is reserved for servicemen," said the woman behind the counter.

"Just the tea, then."

"Got a cup?"

Faber was surprised. "No, I haven't."

"Neither have we, chum."

Faber contemplated going into the Great Eastern Hotel for dinner, but that would take time. He found a pub and drank two pints of weak beer, then bought a bag of chips at a fish-and-chips shop and ate them from the newspaper wrapping, standing on the pavement. They made him feel surprisingly full.

Now he had to find a chemist's shop and break in.

He wanted to develop his film, to make sure the pictures came out. He was not going to risk returning to Germany with a roll of spoiled, useless film. If the pictures were no good he would have to steal more film and go back. The thought was unbearable.

It would have to be a small independent shop, not a branch of a chain that would process film centrally. It must be in an area where the local people could afford cameras (or could have afforded them before the war). The part of East London in which Liverpool Street station stood was no good. He decided to head toward Bloomsbury.

The moonlit streets were quiet. There had been no sirens so far tonight. Two Military Policemen stopped him in Chancery Lane and asked for his identity card. Faber pretended to be slightly drunk, and the MPs did not ask what he was doing out of doors.

He found the shop he was looking for at the north end of Southampton Row. There was a Kodak sign in the window. Surprisingly, the shop was open. He went in.

A stooped, irritable man with thinning hair and glasses stood behind the counter, wearing a white coat. He said, "We're only open for doctor's prescriptions."

"That's all right. I just want to ask whether you develop photographs."

"Yes, if you come back tomorrow—"

"Do you do them on the premises?" Faber asked. "I need them quickly, you see."